'There's All Sorts Of Things We Can Do To Entertain Ourselves.'

Kyle said, licking his smile.

Lauren *was* twenty-seven. She knew he was being verbally clever, saying things that were salacious— Well, maybe he was a gentleman and was *not* salacious. Maybe he meant exactly what he said, and it was only her own wild and wicked libido that was berserk.

How did one know?

She could ask him. *Are you being salacious?*

If she did, he'd probably not understand and be shocked by her assumption.

She was going to have to be clever and slow in order to lead him into allowing her access to his body...

Dear Reader,

Now that winter is well and truly over, we certainly shouldn't get any more snow this year. But in *The Texas Blue Norther* by Lass Small, Lauren Davie has the misfortune to be caught in a snowstorm in Texas! The good news is that she ends up trapped with a particularly sexy rancher—Kyle Phillips—this month's MAN OF THE MONTH.

Eileen Wilks' heroine, Sophie, woke up in the bed of an irresistible stranger in *The Loner and the Lady*. Perhaps most alarming for poor Sophie was that she couldn't remember who *she* was, let alone recognise rugged Seth Brogan!

The final TEXAN LOVER is *That Burke Man* by Diana Palmer. Todd Burke accepts the challenge of saving Jane Parker's ranch—and capturing her heart. In *Seducing Hunter*, the second of the THREE WEDDINGS AND A GIFT mini-series by Cathie Linz, Gaylynn was desperate to get exactly what she wanted—Hunter. And who could blame her, because after all those years he was still as gorgeous as ever.

Lastly, find out what one heirloom cradle does for Duncan Tallchief's love life in *The Cowboy and the Cradle* from Cait London, and don't miss *A Wilful Marriage* by Peggy Moreland—it's a new spin on the 'marriage of convenience' theme that we all enjoy so much.

Have fun!

The Editors

The Texas Blue Norther

LASS SMALL

SILHOUETTE Desire®

*All the characters in this book have no existence outside the imagination
of the author, and have no relation whatsoever to anyone bearing the
same name or names. They are not even distantly inspired by any
individual known or unknown to the author, and all the incidents are pure
invention.*

*All Rights Reserved including the right of reproduction in whole or in
part in any form. This edition is published by arrangement with
Harlequin Enterprises II B.V. The text of this publication or any part
thereof may not be reproduced or transmitted in any form or by any
means, electronic or mechanical, including photocopying, recording,
storage in an information retrieval system, or otherwise, without the
written permission of the publisher.*

*This book is sold subject to the condition that it shall not, by way of trade
or otherwise, be lent, resold, hired out or otherwise circulated without the
prior consent of the publisher in any form of binding or cover other than
that in which it is published and without a similar condition including this
condition being imposed on the subsequent purchaser.*

*Silhouette, Silhouette Desire and Colophon
are registered trademarks of Harlequin Books S.A.,
used under licence.*

*First published in Great Britain 1997
Silhouette Books, Eton House, 18-24 Paradise Road,
Richmond, Surrey TW9 1SR*

© Lass Small 1996

ISBN 0 373 76027 2

22-9704

*Printed and bound in Great Britain
by Mackays of Chatham PLC, Chatham*

LASS SMALL

finds living on this planet at this time a fascinating experience. People are amazing. She thinks that to be a teller of tales of people, places and things is absolutely marvellous.

Other novels by Lass Small

Silhouette Desire®

Tangled Web
To Meet Again
Stolen Day
Possibles
Intrusive Man
To Love Again
Blindman's Bluff
*Goldilocks and the Behr
*Hide and Seek
*Red Rover
*Odd Man Out
*Tagged
Contact
Wrong Address, Right Place
Not Easy
The Loner
Four Dollars and Fifty-One
   Cents
*No Trespassing Allowed
The Molly Q
†'Twas the Night
*Dominic
†A Restless Man
†Two Halves
†Beware of Widows
A Disruptive Influence
†Balanced

†Tweed
†A New Year
†I'm Gonna Get You
†Salty and Felicia
†Lemon
†An Obsolete Man
A Nuisance
Impulse
Whatever Comes
My House or Yours?
A Stranger in Texas

Silhouette Christmas
   Stories 1991
'Voice of the Turtles'

Silhouette Spring
   Fancy 1996
'Chance Encounter'

*Lambert Series
†Fabulous Brown Brothers

One

It all began quite stupidly when the car phone gave its rude beep.

Lauren Davie was by then a mature twenty-seven. She didn't instantly reply to intrusions. She was driving out west of San Antonio, there in TEXAS, and she just wasn't curious who would be calling.

Whoever was calling on the phone gave up. There was only the hushed song of the tires touching on the asphalt. And the wind blew, trying to tumble the portion of loose blond hair that wasn't protected by her white golf hat.

With the car top down, she was vulnerable to the winds. She loved it. There was a feeling of freedom, of escape, to drive alone in the breezes under the sun.

But she wore driving gloves. Her golf hat with its long bill was enough shade for her face. Of course, she wore a silk blouse with long sleeves, and her silk trousers covered her legs. The silks were colored in pale shades of sand.

Her car was cream colored. The top was white.

As Lauren drove along, the radio music was interrupted. She learned there was a warning of an approaching storm.

She looked around at the uninhabited area. The trees were discreetly low. The sky was clear. The surface of the land was uneven so that it wasn't boring. The wind was gentle if one was still. At the speed she was going, with the car's top down, the wind was searchingly frisky and intrusive.

The sun above her was obvious and it was not screened by storm clouds. It was a perfect March day. The bluebonnets were like jewels strewn across the land in blue magic.

Lauren Davie was restless. She didn't know what was wrong with her life. She had everything she wanted. Why was she so disgruntled? What could she target in her life with criticism?

She was busy. She helped out at the hospital and the food bank. She had almost too many friends. Those same friends were trying to marry her off. Lauren wasn't interested in being married and nailed down. What an expression.

Because one great-grandmother had been especially frugal, Lauren had her own money and was free. She didn't need a job. She volunteered her time. She probably needed to start a business.

What sort of business? What—really—interested her enough to apply her attention to what endeavor?

Nothing she could think of at that time. If she put her mind to it, something would appeal to her. She'd make a good CEO. She would let everybody else run the whole shebang.

If everyone else ran the business, what would she do? How would her life be any different from what it was? She'd have even more money.

Her thinking was out of whack. She needed to concentrate on something that was interesting enough and stimulating enough and ragged enough that her attention wouldn't wander.

Yes.

Of course.

Right away.

The turnoff from the highway ought to be somewhere along that particular empty stretch of the two lane road. It would be to the right and go north. Her eyes watched with some discontent.

An interestingly weird portion of her friends was taken with the game of a pretend insurrection and how to cope if the government was taken over by an enemy. To Lauren, it seemed somewhat juvenile.

She thought such an exercise was rather similar to an adult version of Dungeons and Dragons. That fascinating lure had come into being with quarter-supplied video games, and later it was the alluring miracle of the 1980's Apple Personal Computers. The Apple computer was matched with the early computer line called the Gorilla Banana, which had the dot matrix printer.

When those had burst into being, Lauren had been quite young. She hadn't been overly interested. But her daddy had thought having the Apple II and the matrix printer would help in schoolwork.

At the time, all the kids had come to her house to see the computer and play with it. It had been an interesting time. The computer had been magic to them all.

And for her, now, to be driving out for an airplane pod drop was really another type of Dungeons and Dragons. The pod was a yellow gourd and it had a long cotton tail tied to it. The tail helped the searchers to see it fall to the ground.

At twenty-seven, wasn't she too old for such games? Not yet.

Lauren had become involved mostly just to get away from the routine of golf, bridge and meetings. These newer, more complicated games were a distraction.

So.

She was admitting she was bored?

Hmmm. Maybe so.

If she was only bored, what was the solution to the boredom?

Her sisters would say it would be something else that was newer. Something more stimulating. Like organizing and helping with some group, traveling and shopping... Or a man.

Searching for something new was why Lauren was driving out in the sticks, looking for a side road in order to go to a pod dropping.

In the pod would be some kind of directions. When it was retrieved, the group would "assault" some way station and conquer whoever had been designated to act as the enemy. The actual taking was benign. No rough stuff.

Well, *some*times the assault got rough. There are just people who take everything seriously—even in games like basketball, golf and cards. There were people who played so intensely that it wasn't a game. It *was* war! So, basically, this pod game was a war.

Take Willard Newman. He was serious about everything. Even her. Willard had wanted her daddy's backing. He didn't just want Lauren Davie, he wanted her daddy to see him as kin. That way Willard would have the backing of a man who had clout.

It seemed to Lauren that no serious courter had ever seen only her. He'd seen past her to her daddy, to the Davie holdings, to security for himself.

Recognizing such a fact was somewhat diminishing.

It could be no surprise that Lauren had become sour about men. She wondered how it would be to see the light in a man's eyes that was for her and not for her money. It would never happen. Her daddy's name was prime in TEXAS. No one could hear her last name was Davie without asking, "He kin to you?"

They'd ask in just that way. Not if she was her daddy's daughter, but was he kin to her.

Sourly impatient with herself, Lauren watched for the turnoff, and it finally came along with the road under her tires. She signaled needlessly. There were no other cars. She turned with skill from the lessons Mr. Soper had given her in driver's training those years ago. And she went on, following the map.

By then, the road wasn't divided by a painted line down the middle. It was just a road. She felt she was far, far away from civilization. Soon the road deteriorated. In TEXAS? A deteriorated road? It was still asphalt.

But that didn't last, either. The road became a one-track, dirt road.

Was she lost? Had she taken the wrong turn? There were no markers. The Good Guys of the exercise couldn't allow the Enemy to know where they were.

Lauren sighed. She carried water with her always in the wide country of TEXAS. And she had the car phone.

What was the name of the road?

There had been a couple of turnoffs that had been dirt tracks, just like this one she was on.

She stopped and looked at the secret map. Lordy, Lordy, deliver her from games. The map was accurate. It showed she was to go straight ahead and she judged she had another mile at least.

How had she gotten tangled up in some game this strange?

Stupidity.

Undiminished by her own labeling, she went on, watching the mile creep on the adjusted odometer. The moving, seemingly undulating land had emptied out. Even the mesquites were scarce, but there was an occasional, lone oak. There were vast ranges and the vista was beautiful, but it was lonely and bare. It was grazed land. There were cattle out there somewhere.

The meeting place was a little past that presumed mile, but there were the other two cars. They were tucked in under the short mesquites that appeared along parts of the roads. The cars were hidden? How droll.

The short, lacy trees were gnarled, and cattle had trimmed up the branches so the trees were like useless, fragile umbrellas. The noisy couple with their mesquite-hidden cars was jubilant she had arrived.

Mark met her and opened her car door. He scolded, "Why didn't you answer your car phone? Melissa

called, she's about to have the baby! So Gail and I are
going back. You can handle this one. Tom and Buzz
couldn't make it. Jack'll be here in no time. He'll buzz
you first, then drop the pod. Thanks, honey. We're
gone!''

And they left.

Lauren sat in her car, watching the other two cars
disappear. She thought, *Why am I here? What on
earth am I doing? This is really dumb. At my age, I
ought to know better than to get involved in something this stupid!*

And there she was, dressed in silks with fragile
shoes. And she was supposed to drawl through the
fence and retrieve the pod?

Disgruntled, she waited.

And waited.

She looked at her watch and sighed. She looked at
her silent car phone. She wondered why she was sitting there.

Eventually, she heard the sound of a small plane.
She looked up. She looked around. She looked down
the dirt road. At some distance, she saw the plane
buzzing the mesquites clear down yonder. That would
be Jack.

Jack had never struck Lauren as being particularly
bright. However, he could fly a plane. She could not.
But if he was that smart, why was he buzzing the mesquites, clear down there?

She had started her engine and was bouncing down
the lane toward where Jack had been. Had he gone on
off a way and was supposedly dropping the pod?
Away from the trees? Why clear out of sight after
buzzing the place to call their attention? He could have
dumped the pod there!

Men are strange.

Something entirely logical to a woman is beyond a man's grasp.

It would seem basic that if a person was going to try to communicate with someone, however secretly, he wouldn't buzz them first and then go on off to drop the pod someplace else, out of sight.

The way he'd flown was right out over that bare, roadless land. The male retrievers had probably thought it would be rugged to then hop out of their cars and trudge off after the damned gourd.

Lauren took a steadying breath.

Then she looked in her glove compartment. Yes. A compass. She removed it. Her father had given it to her. He was another strange male. In this, her daddy had been right. For the first time since she was sixteen and passed her driver's tests and had a car, she did need a compass. How had her daddy known such a time could come?

He'd probably understood that she would get entangled with some males whose idea of excitement was to go out onto the wide and empty land and find a plane-dropped gourd. How had her daddy known?

Well, he was male.

And with that revelation, Lauren recalled her mother sighing and mentioning just that very thing! 'He is a man,' she'd say. And until that very minute, Lauren had always thought her mother had been bragging and complimenting her husband, who was Lauren's daddy. But her mother's evaluation was a sobering thought. Her father was a man.

The compass confirmed that, as the plane had disappeared over the uneven land, it had been five degrees west of North. Okay. There was no way her car could go through that barbed wire fence and out over that land. A Jeep would have had less trouble.

So Lauren took a Great Forbearing Breath, got out of her car and began to follow a plane. She was doing that! Perhaps there is some comment that could be made about women. Why was she there?

She held the compass in her hand and at the top of the rise, she looked to see which way the plane had turned.

The plane was . . . gone.

Yes.

So Lauren looked for the trailing cloth that was to identify the pod. And other than the grazed and uneven land with a few rocks and a whole lot of sky, she could not see one damned thing.

It is depressing to be involved with unskilled people. Amateurs.

Obviously, Lauren Davie was included in that evaluation.

She stood at the top of the rise and examined the ground that had been under the plane. It was then she became aware the wind was blowing. She was no longer in her car with the top down. But the wind was blowing.

She took a handful of the sparse grasses and tossed them up. The wind was strong. She would have to look to her right of the plane's path . . . about ten additional degrees?

She put the compass on North and walked ten degrees to the right. She saw nothing.

Lauren was a dedicated woman. She would find the damned pod. She trudged along, watching so avidly that she didn't look up at the darkening sky.

With her intentness, it was some time before she realized the sun was gone. There was no friendly shadow accompanying her. She looked at the sky with some indignation. From where had all those dark clouds come?

And she shivered. Could the weather people be right?

Silk is a marvelous material, but even silk has its limits. Her raincoat was in her car. Her car was...that way. She had to find the damned gourd-pod.

So she searched.

And she *found* it! It was not with glee or satisfaction that she lifted it from the ground. It was with grim, teeth-clenched determination.

The tricky wind had played with the pod as it had fallen. It was not where it should have been, which was right...where?

Lauren stood and looked around, holding the damned cloth-tailed pod. She looked at her compass. She pointed it North...and she began to walk back the allotted degrees to her right.

She walked at an angle. She would find the car. She would never go on another pod hunt in all the rest of her life. She hoped Mark's wife had triplets.

It took some time for Lauren to realize she could possibly be lost. She figured if she went south and west, she would find the line of mesquites. From there, she would find her convertible. The car was not only hidden among some mesquites, but she had left it with its top down...and rain or dust or something was approaching.

It was not turning out to be a good day.

She would survive...even this. She would find the convertible before she really, really needed the raincoat in the back seat. She would.

The sky darkened almost to night and the winds were not nice.

Lauren trudged along carrying the gourd-pod, which was gaining weight with every step. She was cold. She shivered violently. Her nipples were terse and pinched, and her skin agreed with the discomfort.

She could handle cold. She would find the car, the coat and put the top up, get in and turn on the heat!

The heat. It would be warm and the stream of the heat would go over her body and soothe her. She had the damned stupid gourd-pod, and she would find her car again.

Lauren lost her hat. It was just—gone! She was freezing. She stopped and wrapped the long pod tail around her. It was only minimally better. She was cold.

And...where was she?

She looked around. It was all so relentlessly the same. Rolling ground. No sun. No stars. No clue as to exactly where she was. The compass said North was that way. She went south.

If only she could just get to some trees...even to mesquites...she would be better off. She was so cold.

Lauren redid the long cloth tail of the pod, wrapping it around her head, her neck, and her chest. Her teeth were chattering.

What was a damned gourd-pod worth? Why had she felt the need to go and find it—all by herself? She would probably die out there. Alone. Her bones would eventually be discovered. By then, it would have been so long, since her death, that the finders would assume she was a relic from long, long ago.

She turned to view the approaching storm and her mind saw a man on a horse. So she was hallucinating. Big deal. She didn't have anything else to entertain her. Lauren's mind had decided she needed to be rescued and her imagination managed to conjure that.

So she turned her back on the foolishness and trudged off—south and a little west.

Behind her, she heard horse's hooves.

Yep. That would go right along with the idea that she was being rescued. Her imagination had always been rather vivid. She'd spent most of her childhood reading and rereading her maternal grandmother's carefully preserved comic pages of Flash Gordon and Prince Valiant.

That grandmother was remarkable.

Lauren figured she was in the final stages of freezing, and she would go out on Prince Valiant's horse. Okay. She could handle that.

Prince Valiant's voice came from behind her. "Hey, where the hell are you going?"

How unprincely. Men *never* acted as they were supposed to act.

She stopped and turned to confront the phantom. "You're *supposed* to step down, take off your hat and sweep a really good bow." With those directions, she stood shivering with her teeth clicking and waited, her back to the storm.

He swung down from the horse with beautiful ease. He took off his coat and wrapped her in it.

That beat the bow all hollow. The coat was gloriously warm. She closed her eyes, knowing she'd already died and probably was in hell. It was so warm.

Well, maybe not hell exactly. She hadn't been *that* bad.

The masculine voice told her, "Get on the horse."

Huh? She was going to hell on a horse? That seemed a nasty thing to do to a horse.

She asked the phantom, "What's he done?"

The phantom's face was sour. He groused, "I hate women. They always do the dumbest things."

Warming inside the coat, she retorted heatedly, "Women? *Women* do dumb things? Do you know that I'm out here for only one thing?"

His interest changed and riveted. "You streetwalking?"

With great, adult patience, she replied, "I came out here with a group to—"

And she couldn't blab a secret club's activities. She was staunch.

"Yeah?" He encouraged her speech with his riveted attention.

Why didn't his Stetson blow away? She was fascinated.

She saw that his shoulders were hunched. He was cold. Where was his coat? It was on her. She said, "I'll give your coat back to you in just a minute. It's so warm."

And he replied nicely but he leaned close as he yelled over the sound of the winds, "As soon as you're just about thawed, we'll get out of here before it thunders."

"It's thundering?" Her eyes got big and her head jerked around.

"It's just wind right now. It'll get interesting in a while. Are you warm enough to get on the horse?"

"What's his name?"

"Whose?"

"This horse." She was kind and pointed to the horse so that he'd know what she meant by the word. She didn't think he was very bright.

But the male creature replied, "Block Head. We just call him plain Block."

She lifted her chin a little. "He seems more intelligent than that." She was chiding.

"He don't know no never mind."

She indicted the horse's position and mentioned kindly, "He's protecting us from the wind."

"That's 'cause he don't know not to."

She stiffened. Then she said in her Daughters of the Alamo voice, "I'm ready to ride."

He smiled and bit his lower lip. She was probably hostile enough now to see to herself. He said, "Give me the coat. I'll wrap you in this here blanket. I'd take the blanket but it don't have no sleeves. Understand?"

He was a basic man. No wonder he had so carelessly referred to streetwalking. He probably didn't know any better. She would be careful of him. She took off the coat with steely discipline.

He took hold of her and tossed her up on the horse. Lauren didn't shriek or sprawl because her daddy had been doing something like that to his daughters all their lives.

She landed neatly in the saddle. She would ride; he would walk. He was a gentleman under all that crudeness. He knew his mann—

"Move your foot out of the stirrup."

He was boarding the horse . . . too.

But he sat in back of the saddle and he shifted until he got the blanket right, covering the front of her and

her legs, then he opened his coat and covered her entirely.

In a sexually stimulating, roughened voice, he
commented in her ear, "It's jest a good thing you got
your own gloves."

He spoke of those thin-skinned, driving gloves,
which protected her hands from sun-browning. Sure.
But thin as the leather was, the gloves were better than
nothing. She said a dismissive, "Yes."

Then he startled her as he said quite naturally, "The
pod's tail makes a pretty good cover for your head and
neck."

How'd he know it wasn't a cantaloupe? She replied
a nothing, "Umm."

He didn't realize the subject had been rejected by
her. He said, "We've found a couple of them there
things. What's in them? Ones we've tried ta see, they
just crumbled."

She looked at the pod, which was the size and shape
of a cantaloupe. "I thought it was a distress signal
from a plane flying oddly." Jack's flying *was* odd.

The man in back of her with his arms around her
said, "He had enough room to land. He didn't need
any such distress signal."

"I guess not." But she did hear in his words that he
had been watching as the plane had buzzed the mesquites and then dropped the pod.

Why had he waited in the beginning of the storm?
Why hadn't he come to her immediately? He'd al-
lowed her to find the pod. He'd known where it was?
If he was so curious, why hadn't he retrieved it first?
She would have never known if it had been found or
lost forever.

This person in back of her on the horse had mentioned they had found other pods. Who all had they told of finding them? Where were the ones they'd found?

This whole adolescent activity was only a confirmation that they were all bored. They had too much spare time with little to distract them. Well, Mike's baby might distract him for a while.

Actually, Mike had had very little to do with his wife having a baby. She'd done all the work. Come to think of it, even at a time when his wife could be very uncomfortably pregnant, Mike had run off on a pod hunt. He had.

She said lazily, "Next time, I get to sit in back."

"The wind's at my back," he said next to her ear. Then his voice was different, lower, huskier. He said, "I'm sheltering you."

She accepted that as only right and asked, "Where are we going?"

"To the nearest house."

She was courteous. "Thank you."

"You're welcome."

It began to rain quite nastily cold and wet. He pulled her head back under his chin, and she was protected. He slid his hand across her ribs below her breasts under the blanket. "You warm enough?"

Her mouth responded in a tiny, female way that was embarrassing. She told him, "My feet are cold."

"Sit Indian-style. I'll balance you."

She was surprised. Here she was countering all her horse training. She was slumped back against a man and now her legs were crossed under the blanket and she was—warm.

He fumbled down her stomach and his hand slid into her trousers. "Oops, sorry. I'm trying to see if your feet're okay."

"They are."

"Good."

A lecher. She squinted a little, as she went over the karate lessons she'd taken because her daddy had insisted. She'd been good at it. She'd nailed the instructor. He'd been hostile to her after that.

If the instructor had gone along the whole way, instead of trying to escape, she would have thought he was letting her win. But he'd tried hard to win over her.

Winning had been heady.

Of course, she'd antagonized yet another male. Her father had laughed.

Her mother had altered the classic, "Never give a man an even break." But her mother had added, "You'd lose."

And she had. By being so confident and physically safe, she'd lost just about every male who'd come down the pike. Even all those who had been blinded by her daddy's clout. She'd lost them all.

Which ones had she wanted?

And lying back against a crude man, she went over all of the contenders like turning pages of a diary, and there hadn't been a one she'd really and truly wanted. To be a twenty-seven-year-old woman who had never really been tempted must be some sort of remarkable record.

She was probably freezing to death and looking back on her life in a farewell. Actually she was warm and cozy, cuddled down, cross-legged but secure on some man's saddle. She was leaning back against him and wonderfully wrapped in his blanket and the shared coat. His right hand was innocently tucked under her left armpit.

His wrist was resting on the top of her breast, which moved with the horse's stride. At least the man wasn't groping her.

She didn't realize his wrist was feeling her. Only hands did that. Not wrists or backs or arms.

Two

The wind was howling and shrill across the empty land. There was nothing to sieve the sound, but it was moaning and serious.

The rescuer had turned the horse away from the storm, so the brunt of the wind was on the man's back. He was Lauren's windshield. That was perfectly logical. Any man protected a woman. It probably started in TEXAS, when there were many, many more men than women, and women were precious.

Of course. Women should always be treated as if they are precious. They are.

The precious woman peeked around from her limited sanctuary. Where were they going? She was so covered that she couldn't see ahead, but she remembered there was absolutely *nothing* ahead of them. They were just drifting as animals drift before a mean wind. That's how cattle piled up against fences or went off bluffs or fell through ice.

She had clear memories of hearing her father raising verbal hell over the stupid cattle who'd done that. He'd been furious! Her mother had listened calmly, seated on the sofa, and watched Lauren's daddy.

The daughters had been sent from the room. Their mother had said to them, "Hush. Run along."

Then when he'd calmed down, and the daughters could hear only the sounds, they would hear their mother's voice.

What had their mother said to their father? What had she done to soothe him? Lauren would have to ask her. Until then, it had been something Lauren had never realized she might need to know.

Her nose was down in the blanket and most of the blanket was surrounded by his opened coat. With all that and the wind, Lauren asked, "What is your name?"

Oddly enough, he understood her. He said in a questioning statement peculiar to TEXANS, "I'm listed in the book as Kyle Phillips? But I answer to just about anything if the caller is serious."

She replied, "How do you do?" And she bowed her head a trifle, as those words had demanded since she'd first been taught the phrase, long ago.

He replied to her response, "Pretty good, so far. What's your name, honey?"

Just the fact that he'd called her 'honey' was a clue. He was basic TEXAN. So she said, "I'm not sure I should give it out in these circumstances."

"It's okay."

He was saying he was safe for her. If he knew her father's name, what if he just decided to hold her for ransom? She could give her first name. "I'm called Lauren."

"Lauren. That's a real nice name."

How strange to have such a conversation with the wind howling around them and the horse patiently plodding along. Occasionally they moved to one side or the other. It was probably done to avoid something.

Warm, her stomach growled. Could she ask if he had some tea and cakes?

She could be flipping out. Dreaming. Hallucinating? Was she actually on a horse riding... "Where are we going?"

"The place is yonder a ways. We'll have a fire."

"In the—place?"

"Yeah."

Now how big could his place be? She said a nothing, "Oh." And she knew full well that everybody in TEXAS called their holdings their "place" because that was where they were. It could be a half acre or it could be miles square. She sighed.

And he heard her defeated sound. "It'll be okay."

Sure it would. Men were not any smarter than women. Their perception of things was unusual and completely different. Even plain, ordinary *words* had other, changed meanings. And then there was sex.

Lauren had found that out when she was quite young. Her cousin Theo had played Doctor with the fascinated Davie sisters. At that age, it was just looking.

Since that introduction by Theo, Lauren had managed to avoid such bold encounters. She was still a virgin.

Theo had gone on to actually become a doctor. Lauren had never gone to him for medical purposes.

Being human was one big pain in the neck, or lower. There were all the rules. All the customs. No other mammal had to fool around with all that stuff. The difference was to prove humans are superior beings.

Even as limited as she was, she could peek around the supposedly virgin land. She wondered what horrific wastes humans had discarded, buried deep in the low, surrounding hills. Were the hills real hills or just earth-covered piles of waste? Animals didn't pollute the world but briefly. Humans really loused it all up. In some places, the pollution would be dangerous for hundreds of *thousands* of years.

How could the people, who lived in that distant future, know? What if the chemical wars wiped out all previous knowledge and future peoples or creatures would have no clue about the dreadful storages of harmful waste?

Being human wasn't a brag.

Being a woman meant you followed all sorts of rules. You either did—or you didn't. Hadn't.

Since Lauren was in the didn't/hadn't category, if she was in the middle of dying, right then, and going to freeze into an ice statue, should she take advantage of this opportunity to know what Life Was All About?

She'd take another look at this person whose name was nicely Kyle Phillips, and she'd decide. Had her guardian angel sent him so that she could experience him? It seemed rather unkind to take advantage of an innocent man.

Of course, he *had* asked if she was a streetwalker. He might not be too difficult to lure.

She lifted her head and therefore straightened her body a bit as she peered around to see if anything was in sight. It was *snowing!*

As she said, "It's snowing in TEXAS!" She became vividly aware that her shift had caused his hand to come free of her armpit and cover her breast! She said, "Sorry," as if that had been her fault.

He put his hand back under her armpit and replied, "My fault."

How kind of him to take her guilt. She would have to pay attention and move more carefully.

She was again discreet. With her head back under his chin, she could smell the freshness of him. Obviously, he didn't smoke. He smelled nicely male and pure. And she began to wonder what he looked like.

As had happened on occasion, she would more than likely be disappointed.

She tried to recall how tall he was and how he looked...really. He was becoming quite nice in her mind. When they got to the Place, wherever that could be, she would be able to see if all her thinking about him was true.

With some tolerance, she considered how like a woman to devise a romance out of absolutely nothing. He'd found some dumb broad out on the land with no means of transport and not dressed for the weather. And he'd managed to get her wrapped up nicely and held warmly.

So her romance novel mind had gone into overdrive, and she was imagining a Hero with a capital H. How could she possibly be so silly?

It was the storm. Her circumstances. And the fact that she would have frozen to death without him, and she was grateful? Yes. Umh-mmm. Mmmm.

Her imagination was really pretty silly. He was silent. He hadn't talked all that much. He looked around and guided the horse. She wouldn't even know he was aware of her being a woman except that his hand had been tugged from her armpit and that hand had curled around her breast.

How cheeky of him to have done that. He had no upbringing. He probably was an orphan and not schooled at all.

If that was so, she might could—use him! She just might do that. She'd be kind but she would see if she could use him. She'd look him over and see if she could endure him—enough. It would be an experiment. Out in the blowing storm that carried a load of snow . . . the snow was getting deep.

She asked, "Are we lost?"

"Not yet."

An interesting reply. Not—yet. Did he plan for them to become "lost" while he had his wicked way with her?

Well, now, Lauren, not every man sees you as a tasty morsel. He probably has five women waiting for him plus a wife and fourteen children.

Or he might not really *care* for women. That could be. Think of a curious woman being in a cabin in a storm with an indifferent man.

Perhaps there would be a TV? She didn't have her purse. It was back in her roofless, exposed and vulnerable car. In her purse was her tatting. Her tatting had saved her sanity any number of utterly boring times.

What did the man behind her look like? The man who was holding her body on the horse with him. He breathed. She could hear him breathe. It was as if keeping her balanced was a chore.

It was interesting that the horse wasn't bothered by the storm. She sneaked a glove-filmed hand from its shelter, leaned forward and brushed the snow from the horse's mane.

Somehow, that jarred Kyle's hand from her armpit again and it was again on her breast. As she stiffened and leaned back, he said, "Sorry."

And he again tucked the hand into her armpit. He had a little trouble, and he had to move her breast over so that he could get his hand where it was supposed to be. But he accomplished that discreetly with his wrist.

Lauren considered thoughtfully that, if he was at all tolerable, he would probably be easy. She would see.

The horse plodded on through the snow. She again asked, "Are we lost?"

And he again replied, "Not yet."

She began to anticipate the line shack. That was what Kyle meant. He would have a line shack somewhere as his place.

She had seen several line shacks in her time of learning to ride. Long riding trips had involved becoming familiar with line shacks. They were neat and tidy and warm. The facilities were primitive but clean. There would be a protected place to rest the horse.

The only fly in the ointment was they might not be alone in the shack. There could be other refugees sheltering from the storm.

With the thought, Lauren began to reason with her guardian angel who was a nuisance at best.

They came to a barbed-wire fence. She glimpsed the fence from the side of her blanket covered face. In TEXAS such fences are called bob wire. When she was little, she thought the fences all belonged to her Uncle Bob. She had been grown before she knew an "r" was in the labeling.

She had never considered having to cope with a fence. She frowned at it. It was tall and securely made. It was five strands instead of the normal three strand indication of property.

Trees were in the distance. That was nice. The horse seemed to be a little perkier. His steps were a bit quicker. Her breasts shimmered somewhat and so did her stomach.

Rock hard Kyle seemed relaxed and indifferent.

The snow became a little heavier. With the fence, the line shack could very well be occupied. Wouldn't that be a snit! Here she was planning a seduction— right after she confirmed that Kyle was worth a one night stand—and now they were getting back to civilization.

How droll to match a barbed wire fence with civilization.

She glimpsed . . . a barn? It was inside the fence. There were horses ahead of them! Where had they come from? Horses never sought shelter unless the storm was severe. There were too many loose horses, and the barn was too big for a line shack.

They were not going to a line shack? How discouragingly disappointing. Well, damn.

This great opportunity for a discreet seduction of a basic man was fizzling. She wouldn't know—anything. She was right back where she'd started. No, she had a topless car full of snow . . . out somewhere on beyond. Which direction? She hadn't kept track.

However, if they'd had their backs to the storm all this time, they were east of her car.

They came to an entrance in the fence, which had a cattle grid. The other horses went over the grid with distaste. Their horse walked over it with familiarity and some interest. No words were exchanged. Kyle was silent. How like a man to do something like this and thwart a willing woman. How snide of him.

Well, he probably wasn't interested in women. Or he could have a lover. He could be committed.

He turned east again after going through the gridded gateway. And ahead, nestled in trees, there was a house.

A whole house.

The horse took them through a second gate. That, too, had the cattle guard and the horse went over it with some frisky movement.

She inquired politely, "Do the round tubes on the grill have electricity in them?"

"No," Kyle responded. "The horse just knows it's going into forbidden territory and he needs to show off."

"Oh."

No one came out to greet them. The place was deserted? It was a big old, old, old house. It was rather elaborate and had been meticulously expanded. It spread as does any place which must house more and more people. How many would be there?

The house had been cared for. It had been repaired and repainted and plumbed. The steps were sturdy.

The front porch was perfect. It had a table and comfortable chairs off to the side, back under the roof of the porch. The porch was on the southeast side of the house. That got the summer gulf breezes.

The northwest was where the storms came with threatening clouds black and mean...and more snow.

There were the leafed pin oaks and the bare-leafed pecan trees and some of the nasty, scrawny mesquites. No one walked barefooted under mesquites. The thorns were mean.

There were not-yet-leafed hackberry trees and barely budding lilac bushes.

And there were bluebonnets. Those precious weeds were a spring flower and the TEXAS state flower.

They really did look like bonnets crowded on a hat rack. And they were blue. But if you looked closely, there was a pink-purple that was accurately put. And there was a perfect cream. That was looking closely. Otherwise, a field of bluebonnets was a marvelous sea of blue and green magic.

Also disappearing under the snow, there were the Indian paintbrushes and the firewheel. There were poppies and buttercups. And the mesquite trees weren't yet leafing out. They're generally the last tree to do that, and they are the biggest natural nuisance in TEXAS.

The oaks' new leaves had pushed off last year's leaves. The trees did that in one day or night. When it happened, it seemed to be all at once. There was the sound like rain as the discarded leaves slithered, sliding down the roofs like heavy droplets.

Lauren looked around, seeing the snowy setting. It was unusually quiet. The snow softened sound. No one came out to see who was there. She asked Kyle, "What is this place?"

He dismounted, and he looked up at her as if judging, then he replied, "It's okay."

He reached up his hands, and she slid sideways into them with long practice. He lifted her down and put her on her feet in the snow.

She had the choice of a barn, which had horses, or a vacant house. "Whose horses are those we saw?"

"Somebody keeps them in the barn?"

And she knew they were his.

So he was an itinerant cowboy? Okay. She watched as he sought a key along the top of a window frame and found it.

She told him, "I hesitate to intrude."

"Nobody's here."

"But what if—"

"The people who owned the place haven't been here for years and years. The last newspaper was 1938."

"Aw."

He looked at her with hooded eyes as he asked, "Why the compassion?"

"My granddaddy told me the thirties were a hard time. The Depression."

"Most survived." He unlocked the door and it squeaked open like something never used.

She paused. "Mice. There'll be mice."

He countered that. "There are three cats. I've seen them."

If the cats had been seen, then it would seem he'd been there before. He was a squatter. He'd just moved in and appropriated the place? A whole lot like he'd appropriated her?

She looked at him. And he watched her back.

She wondered: Had he watched her with the pod and decided since she was alone that he could woman-nap her? She looked at him more closely. He wasn't bad. Average height, black hair, green eyes and a square jaw. His shoulders showed he worked hard. He had muscles. His eyes on her were steady and seemingly benign.

He didn't look like a highwayman. Now why would she think about a highwayman? A robber? His clothing was normal and not patched. Therefore he made enough that he could buy clothing.

He'd had such clothing on when he'd found her. He hadn't had to rush to this place to change in order to look normal. He wasn't normal. Kyle Phillips would never look only *normal* anywhere!

She asked, "Do you . . . bunk . . . here?" She should have thought out what she was going to say and how to say it less intrusively.

He replied, "It's my place."

His place. Yeah. Sure. However, if he was there, and stayed there and wasn't thrown out, he might be able to buy it at a tax sale. She wondered who owned the land. Her dad would know. She'd ask.

She inquired, "Been here long?"

He looked at her seriously but with tolerance. He replied, "Long enough."

"Does your phone work?"

He nodded, "In the kitchen." And he moved his hand to indicate the way.

She looked around the entrance hall's exits as she put the gourd-pod on a table. She asked, "Which way?"

"Sorry. I forget manners. Come thisaway."

And he escorted her to the kitchen. There, they could hear the roar of the storm and from the windows they could see the snow blinding their view out and away.

She lifted the phone and with the storm, she was surprised there was the tone. She dialed direct with her card's number and got the housekeeper, who asked, "Yeah?"

Such a jewel had flaws. The rest of her was superb. "Hi, Goldilocks, this is Lauren."

"Yeah, Lorry?"

"I'm safe and sound. The storm's going to delay my returning home. I'll call back later when I know more."

"Okay." And Goldilocks was gone.

Now, why hadn't she asked Lauren questions which could be succinctly, privately answered. Like: "Where are you?" "Are you there by choice?" Stuff like that?

The "I'm safe and sound" should have been a clue. Help these days was too tunneled. Goldilocks was a miracle of a cook. She went through the house with a finger over and along everything to see to it that the cleaning staff didn't miss a thing. But she was no detective. She was too blatant to understand clues.

Goldilocks would tell Lauren's mother that Lauren called and she was just fine.

No alarm would be sounded. After all, Lauren was now twenty-seven and an independent adult. After Kyle had had his wily way with her, she'd probably be dropped down an abandoned well.

She looked at her host. He looked too benign to drop anyone down a well. She asked, "Do you have any abandoned wells around here?"

He replied right away, "I'll check it out."

That made her skin goose bump so that her nipples peaked tightly.

He asked, "Are you any kind of a cook?"

And she replied using her Daughter of the Alamo reasoning, "I only taste."

"Your mother's not doing her part."

"She makes up the...menus." She almost said they had help. He would then ask her father for more money to release her. She added, "We, the children, do the cooking."

"So, you're trained to cook?"

"No. I pour the pan milk and . . . deal out the oat-meal."

He coughed.

She looked out at the snow.

The silence crackled and popped. She said, "The bluebonnets will freeze."

"Are you cold?"

"The blanket—"

"I'll put a fire in the . . . parlor?"

"Please."

"Are you hungry?"

"It's been a while since breakfast."

"You eat lunch?"

"Don't you?"

"I don't always have the time. But when I eat, I eat."

She nodded to agree his words made sense.

He bowed his head and rubbed his nose. He said earnestly, "I'll build a fire in the parlor."

"Thank you." She asked, "Is the water in the sink drinkable?"

He gestured openly. "Gen-u-wine artesian, the real McCoy. Have some."

He went and turned on the faucet and water gushed forth. Lauren had forgotten her parched mouth. She drank two glasses. She put the again-filled glass aside.

"You was thirsty."

And she replied, "Obviously."

He said it earnestly, "You can get any more any-time you want some."

"Thank you."

And he responded with great courtesy, "You are most welcome."

It was then she realized he varied his speech. He might not be a hayseed after all. That only proved he was tricky.

She considered him. How come he was talking thataway? What was his purpose to pose as something other than what he was? He was a coyote.

The animal coyotes are clever and sly. They are amused by their tricks. There are humans who are called coyotes. Like those who smuggle people over into the States from Mexico and charge outrageous prices to guide them. And those intruders who get lost, get lost. And they die in the unpeopled areas from the heat and from not finding water.

Kyle asked, "So you don't cook at all?"

"Oatmeal."

"Then when you get hot, come in the kitchen and I'll get you dinner."

She responded, "Excellent. I'm quite hungry."

"This'll be a ball and a banquet." He almost smiled.

"I'll look forward to it."

And he left the room.

She shed the blanket and went looking for the lavatory. She found one and it was pristine.

Kyle was probably a cattleman but who had cleaned the lavatory? He didn't look the type to care.

She washed her hands before she left that room and got back by the fire before she heard Kyle whistling in the kitchen.

Her daddy whistled. It was such a cheerful sound. Her daddy had told her all cattlemen whistled or sang. It was for the beeves.

Kyle wasn't with cattle, he was in the kitchen fixing her supper. She could set the table. The house was really quite comfortable. There must be a means for heating it.

Lauren found the kitchen and looked at it with untried eyes. She saw that it wasn't like the one at home that was ruled by Goldilocks.

She asked the man by the stove, "May I help?"

He turned and looked at her.

Something happened in her stomach and to her breathing. He was absolutely glorious! Or maybe it was the mouth-watering smell of cooking onions? Something was wobbling her.

He looked at her without the blanket. She wore the soft silk, sand-colored outfit of blouse and trousers. They were more for a drawing room than a kitchen. On her, they were something.

Maybe the something that was so eye-catching was the body inside the silks. With some resolve, he tore his eyes from her and said, "Yes."

He had been agreeing that she was special.

She assumed he meant she could help. So she sought the right cupboards and brought the germane dishes and glasses to the table. But she put them aside. Then she dampened a towel and wiped down the table quite well.

After that, she set the silver precisely, then the plates and glasses. She found napkins. They were yellowed, but fairly clean. In the hall, she found a bouquet of dried flowers and leaves. It was intact, and it was glorious to put it on one side of the table.

He watched her as he cooked. She amazed him. She rattled him. And her body drove him tilted off center.

Her mouth did, too. Her hands. Then she licked her lips!

He breathed . . . carefully.

She asked with courtesy, "What are we having?"

He looked at her a minute as if surprised she could get out a communicating sentence. He finally told her, "Beans. The onions in them are the vegetables. The chili peppers get rid of worms."

She looked aside as she assimilated the last part. She looked at him again and inquired, "Worms? In the house?"

He tilted back his head as he bit his lower lip. His eyelashes almost closed over the humor, and he said, "The ones in your digesting tract."

And she formed her lips thoughtfully as she responded, "Oh."

He went on cheerily stirring the beans and dropping in the onions and peppers.

She noted the beans had come from a can. They would be perfectly all right. He was a sham. She would figure something to pay him back for his sly humor.

She looked in the cupboard and then the freezer and found tortillas. She thawed and toasted them. Then she cut cheese into bits with some of the onions and rolled those into one of the tortillas. Hot, the cheese melted, and she handed him one.

It was perfect.

Actually, it was normal. It was just that they were so hungry that it didn't matter what condition the food was in, it would be good.

Three

In the pantry, Lauren found some dried fruits and washed the various kinds before she cut them up with an apple for a fruit salad. It was pretty and colorful on the plate with the yellow cheese on the tortillas, along with the brown beans and the red peppers.

As they ate, she was leery of the peppers and her fork discreetly isolated them from the beans. The rolled tortillas substituted for bread. They were heated and the cheese melted just right. The milk was from a great glass canning jar. The substance tasted like milk.

Kyle turned on the radio, and they got the weather station. The snow would be a three day deluge according to their information. Settle in and enjoy! That was their advice.

Lauren asked, "Can you ignore the cattle?"

He replied logically, "The beeves are drifting from the storm so the men are guiding them so that they don't get piled up or fall off anything along the way."

Then he added with ease to explain himself, "The milk cows have to be milked but they're here. The horses don't mind a little snow. The Jeep doesn't, either. You wanna go home?"

She didn't. Oddly enough, she didn't want to go home. She said, "I'll have to retrieve my car." And she left the subject hanging. He could figure it out. She wasn't of any mind to go off and leave there. She was going to have an adventure... with him. It would be a first time and with a stranger. If she loused up or quit in the middle of it, no one would ever know.

How strange that a coward like she would come to this rash decision.

Was it being twenty-seven? Was that what was making her so reckless? That and the fact he'd made no real intrusions, uh, he'd kept his hands to himself. Yes, he had. Other than those two times when his hand had slipped out from her armpit.

Where would she sleep? Would he brusquely insist that she sleep with him? Maybe. And maybe she'd just find out what sex was like. She was old enough. She was *beyond* being old enough. Even Sid had had one.

Lauren had noticed that the knowledgeable women's eyes were smug and different. They giggled and whispered. Lauren felt out of it. The last women's golf tournament at the club had been a trial until she was put in with three other women—and not one of them had mentioned anything about any man! It had been a surprise. It had been quite refreshing.

If there were women who... didn't and didn't even talk about it, then why was Lauren Davie so anxious to experience something so private with a total stranger?

She had no idea. But it was something to think about. Something to decide about. What would happen if she just up and told Kyle she was curious?

Would he say, "Okay." Or would he back off with his hands up to fend her off?

She smiled at the idea of his fending her off.

He asked, "What's so funny?"

And she raised her eyes to his and smiled.

"What you thinking?" But he was a little tense as if she was thinking about him and laughing *at* him. That was interesting to observe. He was vulnerable.

She said, "I was playing golf with some women and they were talking. It was just a joke I remember."

"What kind of joke?" He was serious.

She was kind. "It was a woman's joke."

And he asked, "About...men?"

And she was gentle. "No. About another woman who couldn't cook at all. Like I am."

His face changed. He was interested. He considered and told her seriously, "You could learn."

"I am really a peanut-butter woman."

And he complimented her. "You did nice with the tortillas and cheese."

She scoffed, laughing. "It was the onions chopped in the cheese that caught your taste buds. You like onions and hot pepper. You're a chili man."

He nodded as he considered her with a nice smile. And he told her, "Yeah."

It was only then, with the exchange, that she understood he was vulnerable, and she couldn't taste him without hurting his opinion of himself.

It was a giant step forward for Lauren to understand that. She had never really thought about other people that way. They could be hurt. The realization of his being vulnerable was sobering.

With the meal finished, Lauren sat back in her chair and sighed. "I was starved. You are a wonderful cook."

He said it quite nicely, "That fruit thing was nice. Pretty." He appeared lost for words, so he declared, "You got a good appetite."

She assumed he meant her table manners. His elbows were on the table. Could she tolerate that? And she considered manners and mores.

He'd saved her neck. He'd rescued her...and horses! The horses that had gone in the barn gate! He'd been rounding up horses! So *that's* why he'd been out there! He had known about the storm and he'd gone out to get his horses!

Of course.

He hadn't just been moseying along. He'd been there for a purpose. That's why he shifted their course a time or two. He had been monitoring the horses.

And by the greatest chance, he had ran into her out there, on foot. Alone. He could have just gone on and left her there. And she was not dressed for, nor capable of surviving, such a storm. But he'd seen her and been committed. He'd brought her back with him, there to the house where he was living.

Anyone can learn manners. He had saved her very life. He was a good man.

So, as any hostess or superior guest does, she asked questions to lure the people at the table into conversation. He was all the people she had around, so she asked him, "How long have you been here?" Then she clarified it, adding, "—at this place."

"About—'bout two years now." He looked at her. Then his attention went back to his plate.

He most assuredly had a good appetite...for food. What about women? Did he have any appetite for—her? How could she nudge him into such a happening?

Her eyes slitted and she studied him. He was apparently oblivious to her distracted, intense study of him. He was just busy with food. He licked his lips and shifted in his chair and—he ate everything left in sight.

If she ate as much as he was devouring, she'd weigh a ton! The doors in their house would have to be widened. But he was lean. She looked at him seriously. His jaw was hard. He could quite possibly be stubborn. Most men were.

The interior of the house was cooling. The storm was sounds of booms and shrill, shrieking winds. The storm's cold was creeping into the house. It seemed as if the very house shivered in that storm's onslaught.

Lauren was aware of the chill. She figured it was just that she'd been starved. Now her blood had all rushed to her stomach to feast on the food she'd ingested. Such greed in a lady was crass.

As she shivered, she crossed her arms to hold herself still. She had been so helpless since she'd met Kyle that she rejected mentioning it was cold in the house. To say so would be rude.

He glanced up at her. "You cold?"

She nodded in shivering jerks.

"You don't dress right. I'll get you a jacket."

He left the table, crossed the room to the door and disappeared. He came back with his sheep-wool lined jacket. "Here," he said to her. "Try this again."

She put it on with such a sigh that her released breath frosted in the kitchen air. The frosted breath proved she was not reacting to anything, it *was* cold in there!

With the jacket around her, she went to the gas oven and relighted it, leaving the oven door open to heat the kitchen.

He watched her. Then he asked, "How'd you know to do that?"

And she replied carefully, "My momma used to do it when we were small and the morning air was cool. Daddy doesn't like a hot house."

Kyle smiled. "Me, neither."

One of those. His rating fell about twenty points. And she looked at him with clearer eyes. He'd be hard and dictatorial. Well, he'd gotten her the jacket.

However, he hadn't taken off his flannel shirt nor the long underwear, the top of which showed under his chin. He'd adjusted her to his options. He hadn't altered his own circumstances. He'd just adjusted her.

Obviously, such conduct in any man was something for a woman to seriously consider.

Lauren considered the whole situation with this stranger. She leaned more to a brief encounter than to a long view of a commitment. Brief with Kyle was probably better. She was learning. No woman could take on the entire man as Kyle was now. He was old enough to be set in his ways. Any woman would have to adjust to him.

The way her mother had adjusted to her father.

How interesting to acknowledge the fact that her mother bent her life, and those of the children, to her husband's rules. She catered to his comfort, to his schedule and even to his variety of peculiarities.

Lauren looked again at Kyle. All's she wanted of him was a single experience. She was curious. He looked healthy and he could be a capable partner. She would leave him alone if he declined.

It would probably be better if she allowed him time to be comfortable with her. She could be specific in what she liked and didn't like so that, if he disagreed, he wouldn't be lured to her, and she would leave him alone.

They were very, very different. She liked San Antonio. It was a good, settled city. He was obviously comfortable out in the sticks.

She liked the events of music, theater, civic doings and meetings. She was a city woman. She was not taken with living isolated on some plot of ground far outside the city limits.

She would be firm in his understanding that any intimacy was simply curiosity and not a commitment.

She would not lure him. He could be shy and unpracticed. She would be matter-of-fact. She would not accost him that very night. She needed to allow him time to get used to her.

So it wouldn't be that night? *Another* night? There had been too many lonely nights. She wanted him . . . now.

That was crass. Just one life-threatening experience, and she'd turned hungry for a man. She'd known him how long? A couple of hours? They'd ridden silently along. They had been sharing a horse, with him holding her on, with his hand under her armpit.

"Armpit" didn't sound romantic. The word was so anatomically clinical.

He sat back in his chair at the kitchen table, and she glanced around for Goldilocks. No one else was there, so Lauren got up and cleared the table.

There was a *dishwasher!* It hadn't occurred to her there would not be one until she actually saw that there was one. She was grateful.

There were dishes in the washer... for how long? That would only invite ants, cockroaches... or—shudder—mice. She rinsed off the dishes and tucked them back into the washer. Neatly assembled, they would wait for a soap wash.

How strange it was that she had begun to review her mother's marriage. She had lived with her parents for twenty-seven years and in all those years she had to have been aware for at least twenty of them. She had observed that it was her daddy who called the shots.

Her mother adjusted. She had adjusted not only herself, but his daughters. With her daddy around, the daughters were quietened. And Lauren again remembered her mother listening to her husband rant and pace. And she remembered later, hearing her mother's soothing voice.

What had her mother done and said to soothe her agitated husband? That was information Lauren needed. How strange not to have inquired before then.

Automatically, since no one else did it, Lauren took the broom and carefully swept the kitchen floor. One did that to avoid ants, cockroaches and mice. One did it precisely and after each meal. While her mother never lifted a finger, unless one of her flowers was ailing, she did see to it that the floor of the kitchen was pristine.

Kyle sat sprawled and silently watched Lauren. What did he see? Or was he so tired that he would watch a fly?

The exercise was good because she warmed enough to unbutton the fleece-lined jacket.

Her mother had recommended and encouraged her children to exercise. That was done with golf, tennis, swimming and cleaning their own rooms. There were times when Goldilocks was not there and the girls had learned to cook. Lauren then learned about oatmeal and setting the table. And they'd learned to clean.

They had complained. They had Goldilocks and her crews. And their mother had chided her children. "If you don't know how it's done, now, how can you see to it later that it's done right when you're on your own?"

One of those irritating questions which was inarguably true. Her mother had a lot of questions which couldn't be countered. The daughters had tried.

What had her mother said to her tempered father in those times when he was upset?

She would ask her mother.

Kyle said, "I have to go milk the cows. I'm late as it is."

"How can I help?" She volunteered because she needed to know him. She needed their acquaintance to flower so that he wouldn't be surprised when she lifted back the bedcover for him. Or if she got into his bed.

He replied to her question, "Stay here. It's warmer. I'll be back."

And he shrugged into a greatcoat and put on the handy Stetson. He went out the back door, closing it quickly before the winds invaded. Then he went across the screened porch, down the snow-covered steps and off to the barn.

What if he got on his horse and just...left? That would cancel her adventure entirely. Think how boring it would be if he just...left her there.

He wouldn't leave his animals. No man did that. He would be back. And she'd be there, waiting for him.

How would he respond? She'd always been the one who'd stopped hands or chided or wiggled away. She'd locked doors when she was visiting. And she'd never replied to soft questions from the other side of a bedroom door. She'd been careful.

How could she now be bold? Pliant. Coaxing. Available. She thought of the encounters in films. It seemed so easy. Of course. The films were of scripts and actors. None of the actors had the criminal court looming in the background.

It was tough for a woman to seduce a man when he was forced to be cautious. She couldn't criticize the cautioning. It had served her well. Men were more careful.

But she was curious. While not the kind of woman who would tease and leave, she wanted to know what it was like. In this time, Kyle probably wasn't a virgin.

And she stopped, wide-eyed and startled. She had no condoms. Well, hell. That eliminated everything she'd planned. How could she have forgotten condoms? Well, she hadn't *planned* to be there trapped in a damned storm!

She sighed and looked out the window at the blowing snow that was eliminating the footprints he had left in the powdered covering. There she was, in the perfect place, with an attractive rescuer—and no condoms. Now that was a bucket of spit.

It seemed no time at all until he returned with two buckets of milk. He put them into a canister on the porch and rinsed the buckets in water. He was precise and efficient.

He came inside, removed his coat, went back to the table and sat down. He leaned back and tilted his chair onto its back legs. He seemed easy and comfortable.

Disgruntled, she cast a glance at Kyle and caught him looking at her hungrily. Hungrily? He *was!* He might not be too difficult—

No condoms.

Just maybe *he* had one? How could she find out without him knowing what she had in mind?

So she'd planned on sneaking up on him? He would have to know sometime. Why not now when the condom panic was vital? How was she to ask? How did a woman who'd not known a man for very long find out if he had any condoms without seeming . . . ready? Or aggressive? Or blatant?

And she remembered Ginger, who just tilted her head to get the guy out of the crowd. He'd followed, and they weren't seen again for two days. That was nine years ago. How strange for something like that to surface at a time like this.

Ginger must have rung a bell in Lauren's conscience because she still remembered the happening vividly. She probably remembered because she was so innocent that what she had seen then had been a puzzle and her mind had filed it under HUH? until now.

But Ginger probably had had condoms in her pocket...her purse...her shoe...she was always ready. Prepared.

Ginger now had three kids and had been twice divorced. Hmmm.

What had Lauren's mother said to Lauren's father those times after he'd been shouting-angry?

And the next morning, he'd be sleepily smiling at the breakfast table, and he'd be gentle and funny. What had her mother done about him?

Kyle got up and turned on the radio. Not to the weather station as Lauren had anticipated, but to music. It was smooth and easy. It was familiar.

Kyle held out his arms to Lauren and said, "Let's try it."

Lauren hesitated. She had had so much dance training that she was leery of his feet. But she did go to him, and she lifted her arms.

He looked down her body in his coat. He smiled. "If we dance, we might warm up." He tilted his head and bit into his lower lip.

What did that mean? He'd jog her around until she took off the coat and then the silks? Hardly. The silks breathed and were comfortable in heat.

He could dance. Now that was a surprise. He released her, put the chairs against the wall, moved the kitchen table effortlessly and put the other chairs to the table before he came back to her. They continued to dance. He was really good. Some of the lyrics were rowdy.

They danced to just about all the kinds of music, including a marvelous romp of TEXAS stomp. Every TEXAN knows how to stomp. The partners laughed.

She had abandoned the coat after some time. She was held tightly against him as he turned her and moved her around the floor. His body was hard against hers.

There was a slow dance, and he held her to him as he breathed. She'd had men who'd danced with her, held her and breathed that way. Was he stimulated? Enough? How could she discreetly inquire if he had a condom?

Being a woman was tough.

The dancing led to talking, and he could talk. He seemed slow. He chose his words. Did he clean them up? Was he so used to talking with men that talking to a woman was a verbal chore? She could handle men's words. Some women she knew said such words quite easily.

On rare occasions, Lauren had even *said* some forbidden words. Not around other people, but under her breath in trying times.

Everybody has trying times. Frustration. Irritation. Exasperation.

She looked up into Kyle's green eyes...his eyes were really green! How amazing. She'd never known any green-eyed men. So she mentioned, "Your eyes are green!"

"Yeah."

Well, he would know the color of his eyes.

He told her, "Yours are brown."

She'd known. So she just smiled.

He mentioned, "Most people I know have blue eyes."

She agreed. "Around here."

"How'd you get brown eyes?" He smiled a little as he waited for her reply.

She explained, "My momma's great granddaddy was brown-eyed."

"And it took all that time to turn up in you?"

She laughed.

He teased, "You got brown-eyed sisters?"

She hesitated just a tad. "How did you know I have sisters?"

"Everybody talks about Paul Davie and his beautiful daughters. Are they all pretty as you?"

Hmmm. So he knew who she was and who was her daddy. That was sobering. It also entirely canceled her anonymous seduction.

She said, "My sisters are prettier. How did you know about us?"

"Like I said, everybody knows you. You walk down Houston Street and people look at you. I was with a guy who knew you. He said hello to you. But you just smiled at him and went on along."

"If I didn't call him by name, I probably didn't recognize him because he thought he saw one of my sisters instead of me."

He turned her in a swirl to the music before he asked, "That happen a lot—getting taken for one of your sisters?"

"All the time."

So he inquired, "Where are you in that bunch of sisters?"

"I'm second oldest."

"And you're not married?" Even *he* thought he was getting a trifle pushy.

She was used to being asked that. She was patient. She agreed readily enough, "Not married."

"Somebody hunting you down?"

And she was forbearing, "No."

He laughed with real humor. Then he chided her. "I don't believe that for a minute."

Bored with the whole collapse of the seduction, Lauren took a patient breath and told him, "On my honor, no man is interested."

He grinned and his eyes were filled with humor. He really tried to smother his amusement but his humor continued without his permission.

With some hostility and a feeling for self protection, she inquired in a rather deadly way, "What could possibly be so funny?"

He chided, "You don't even see all the guys who yearn after you."

"Balderdash."

"You're like my momma with mice," he explained kindly. "She doesn't 'see' them in the fall when they come inside. That way the mice don't upset her." He turned her to the music with some skill.

"Upset." Lauren rolled the word on her tongue as she tasted it in a narrow-eyed manner.

He didn't recognize hostility and explained logically, "My momma doesn't like mice. Pretending not to see them is her defense."

So curiosity nudged her to ask, "What happens— with the mice?"

Aggressively, but within the limits of dancing, he walked her backward across the kitchen as he replied, "My brothers and I go clean them out of the house. My sisters are a whole lot like my mother."

"How many of you are there?"

He turned her carefully so that she didn't hit the opened oven door. "In numbers? Just five. Like you all."

"And...where are you in the lineup?" She found she was curious.

He was concentrated on a slight dip and turn. He told her, smugly serious, "Top dog. I was first."

Yeah. And he probably ruled them all. He was the pushy type. She found herself saying, "I don't believe I've thanked you for rescuing me from the storm."

He shook his head. It had scared him when he realized she was lost. "I was rounding up the horses. I almost missed you dressed in that sand color like you are."

She had to thank the gods for his horses. If he hadn't gone for them, she'd have frozen.

So he'd had reason to have gone out there. They'd dropped the pod on his land?

As if his thinking paralleled hers, he asked, "What's in the gourd-pod you chased down?"

How had he known only she had chased down the pod? How long had he been aware of her? "I have no idea."

He turned her with some élan. "Who'll open it?" His question was casual, but he was then silent as he waited for her reply.

"Somebody else."

He moved her backward. "I'm curious."

With a shrug she told him, "It's like Dungeons and Dragons." She'd blurted it before her carefulness took hold.

"A game?"

And she could be honest. "Yes."

"Who gets the pod?"

"I'll be called."

"I'm really curious," he said with interest. "Will you tell me about this?"

And she asked, "Are you really renting this land and this house, or are you just here?"

He smiled and twirled her gently as the music stopped. "This is my land."

"Tell me your full name."

"I'm really and truly actually Kyle Phillips. This land was a part of the old Turner estate?" The TEXAS questioning statement. "I was there, at the auction, and I got the bid on this part. It is exactly what I wanted. I know this place."

She asked, "How much land did you get?"

"Enough."

"And you have milk cows?" she questioned.

"Cows are a good cash means." He was watching where their steps took them in the limited room.

She realized he was speaking differently again. "Where's your po' boy language?"

"I was trying to see if you knew me."

"From—?"

And he told her quite easily, "When you were Queen of the Fiesta, I was one of your escorts."

"Really?" The Fiesta was a week-long celebration of spring. There was a parade called the Battle of the Flowers with decorated floats and marching bands.

He guessed, "But you've forgotten me."

She shook her head with a big sigh. "I was petrified."

"Why?"

"I'm not the Queen type at *all!*"

He asked with logic, "Then why did you accept it?"

She shrugged. "Daddy."

"He got you in?" The questioning statement.

"Yes."

And for some reason, he pushed it. "But it wasn't your idea?"

"Never. I'm a shrinking violet."

He laughed. "All shrinking violets go alone out into empty land looking for pods."

"I was bored."

"What . . . stimulates you?"

She shrugged. "By now, not much." Well, actually, he did, but a lady doesn't mention such things. And since he knew who she was and who her family was, any idea of seduction was useless. The whole shebang was a lost idea, a thwarted temptation.

Disgruntled, she thought it could have been such an adventure, with him. Such an interesting time. Now the whole scenario was lost.

She became a little wistful. Her eyes were sad.

"What's wrong?" His voice was earnest.

She looked up in surprise. No one had ever asked that of her before then. How was she to reply without spilling her guts and all the family secrets? What— family secrets? Well, her daddy's ambition for them. Her grandmother's push for their work in social endeavors. Her mother's calm regard.

Distracted, she turned away from Kyle. It wasn't easy being in the Davie family. It wasn't easy being a female who was up for grabs by ambitious men who wanted to elevate themselves with Davie backing.

Her family was picking at her to decide on a husband. By now, more and more of the men over her age were married. Now those bringing her flowers and looking around to greet her father were more her own age and two were younger and looking past her at her younger sisters.

It was a nuisance being a woman. Or was it all just because she was a daughter of her father?

She considered Kyle. How had he happened to be where she needed him so handily? Had he bribed the others to leave her there alone? How had he known about the pod? Had he paid Jack to miss the drop area? By then, Lauren had survived so many clever plots to lure her into nets that she couldn't be surprised by anything.

How could she ever know if a man married *her* and not her father's clout? Such a thought was diminishing to a woman.

She broke gently from Kyle's arms and went to a window to look out on the storm. There was one inside her, too.

Four

Kyle said, "How about some cribbage? We can play here in the kitchen where it's warm."

Lauren smiled. "I haven't played cribbage in a hundred years!"

He put a hand to his chest and exclaimed in hambone exaggeration, "I had no idea you were older than a hundred."

She confessed, "It's the modern makeup."

He nodded as he looked at her and his smile was just under his skin. He went into another room for the playing cards and pegboard. On the round kitchen table, he set up the cribbage board and put the pegs in the middle. "I'm very good at this. How are your hundred-year-old eyes?"

She was smug. "My eyes are like a hawk's."

He sighed in defeat as he said, "I'll probably lose the game."

"More than likely," she responded with smug cheerfulness.

And they played very competitively. They objected and groaned and laughed nastily. How interesting that two such opposite people could spend an evening so innocently.

She was especially surprised. She was sure the game only delayed him. When he'd gotten her on his horse, he *had* groped her. Of course, she had thought it was an accident by whom she'd thought was an innocent man. She recalled his hands' slippings quite vividly. Even then he'd known who she was! How dared he grope her daddy's daughter?

She speculated as to whether his plot to isolate her was to compromise her. After the storm released their isolation, did Kyle think her daddy would bless her marriage to him?

Over her dead body.

With her mind going eighty miles an hour, she played the cards with complete honesty. It was a genetic curse to be honest.

Kyle was tricky. She had to watch every move he made. When he advanced his peg on the board, she had to be sure he hadn't sneaked in another hole or two. Once he'd tried for three holes extra.

And he'd laughed!

She told him quite seriously, "How could I trust you in anything now that I know how you play cribbage?" And she watched him.

He grinned. "This is money-free cards. In anything else, I'd play it straight."

She regarded him in silence. Her face was serious. She asked in a level way, "Would you?"

And he looked up at her with some interest. "On my honor."

But she then asked, "How good is your...honor?"

He shrugged as he looked at her. Quite easily, he told her, "It's pristine."

With some irony, she mentioned, "Your language has changed considerably since my arrival here."

His smile came slowly as he watched her. He admitted, "I was testing you."

"And now? You're cheating, so you are still... testing?"

"No. I've been teasing you."

And she questioned, "You're cheating so that I can trust you?"

He was easy. "You would know the difference."

"Would I?"

"Of course!" He was puzzled and serious. "We're only playing cards. No money. No honor. No rules."

"No...rules."

He put down his cards and folded his arms along the table in front of him. "What's that 'no rules' mean?"

And she replied coolly, "I understand."

"And what is it you 'understand' about?"

She gestured openly, hiding nothing, saying it exactly. "Your game and your—adjusted—rules?"

He shook his head and looked at her seriously. "No."

She tidied her cards, lifted the pack and lay her cards underneath them. "I believe I will find a place to rest. Thank you for the supper. You're an excellent cook."

He rose from his chair. "I'll show you to your room."

Yeah. She said levelly, "Just point. I can find it okay."

"The lights are out." He gestured.

"And how would you know that?" She lifted her chin.

"The refrigerator went off."

She looked around. Hmmm. She mentioned, "The stove is still on."

He nodded once to agree. "It's gas. The house could become quite cold with the storm. I'll build a fire in the living room fireplace. Those sliding doors close, and it'll stay warm enough there, too. You can have one sofa. I'll take the other."

Share a room with him? So he could keep an eye on her? How would she ever escape his probable animal lust?

She considered her plight. It was exactly that . . . a plight. While her mind was stern and logical, there was something very wrong with her errant body. It had behaved quite well in all the years she'd shared it, but now it was in revolt with her brain.

Her attitude was stern and staunch.

Her body was a writhing mass of want. How vulgar of it.

But the really startling bit came when her logical mind said through her shocked lips, "Why not?"

Kyle smiled. He busily went to structure the slow-burning night fire in the living room.

Lauren was appalled. If she could still be appalled, it must be her conscience against her mind and her distracted, wicked, restless, squirming body!

Who would ever believe she could be so out of control? A strict and staid person who had rubbed shoulders with loose women and not only had not understood them but had been unaffected? One who had avoided interested men for so long? How could her discipline so suddenly collapse? Kyle knew her family. He knew who she was!

This could become a study for her master's degree. She ought to keep notes. She looked over at Kyle.

He was watching her very like the eyes of the predators on TV's Nature studies. On those programs, all anyone could see were hungry eyes . . . and fleeing victims.

She was . . . a . . . victim . . . of a greedy man . . . in a snowstorm. Little Nell of the silent films? She?

How many women had Kyle had that he knew enough to be that greedy? He looked on her as a bear after a honeycomb. He would make his move soon now. He would begin to gather the honey to himself. Her.

And down deep in her there was the most startling reaction to the very *idea* of being his honey and being consumed by him!

Well, he wouldn't actually eat her, but he would use her for his body's pleasure. Oh, yes. Her breaths changed to pants.

Then her conscience scolded her brain and her body. *You really don't know this person well enough to be this way. Behave!*

And she recognized the sound. That caught her concentration. She'd heard just that lecture before then! She had a monitor inside her, implanted in her conscience, that was triggered by the excited part of her body! She did! That damned monitor had interfered before!

She narrowed her eyes as she recalled one of those times. She was twelve, and Phillip had her in the garage. He was about sixteen. Why, she remembered that! She had on a dress. She'd always worn jeans or shorts.

He'd told her once that he liked dresses better than pants. That was a clue, so she'd worn a dress to please him.

Around the others, he hadn't acted pleased. He'd hardly looked at her, but the time came when Phillip had lured her into the garage, to see the doodlebug holes, he'd said. She'd been very interested . . . in the doodlebugs.

She'd seen doodlebugs all of her life up until then. Doodlebugs are no big deal. But she was there with Phillip and excited that he'd chosen her to go with him to see the little dirt funnels. He wanted to be with her.

So, not having one clue, she had squatted down and taken a leaf and brushed a bit of dirt into a doodlebug trap. With acquired skill, she made it appear the leaf was a careless little ant. As the bits of earth went into the hole, the waiting doodlebug kicked dirt over it to entrap the foolish ant.

Phillip had squatted beside her—and he was *naked!* Where were his clothes?

How had he done that so quickly? Why was he naked?

Lauren was so mature at twelve and had such control that she hadn't—looked. That had taken some discipline for a budding woman who lived in an overwhelmingly female household. She'd asked, "What are you doing?" She was curious as to why he'd taken off his clothes.

He'd replied, "You'll like it."

Now, how many times had she heard the very same line since then? It seemed to Lauren that every male was taught that line from puberty. Maybe even before then.

But, being as she was, and quite literal, when Phillip had said they were going to see the doodlebug traps, she hadn't considered any sidelines. Like sex.

They had stared at each other, then they heard the arriving sisters and friends coming toward the garage.

Phillip had instantly disappeared.

Coming through the side door of the garage and seeing Lauren, her sisters had logically asked, "What are you doing in here?"

And she'd been honest. "Phillip wanted me to see the doodlebug holes."

They'd looked around. Phillip was nowhere. Then they looked back at Lauren. They had laughed. They'd thought her reply was a tease. They hadn't believed her.

But her older sister, Millie, had said, "You're just a bit literal. Come on, before you get in trouble."

But all that had gone right over Lauren's head. She thought Millie meant Joe would be cross with them being in the garage with his cars, because one of them might put a bare hand on a polished fender. Joe was responsible for the cars and he was excessively picky. No one had permission to go into his garage.

So since then, Lauren had noted the term, "You'll like it" was universal. It was a preliminary. It was staid. She'd heard it many times after Phillips' try.

Now here was this probably fake cowboy who claimed to know her family. He was saying she'd "like" it if she slept in the living room with the fire going in the fireplace and him on the other sofa. Yeah. Sure.

But she *was* curious.

How was she to handle this?

She could say, *I've always been curious, shall we?*
She *was* curious. So why not?

But she wasn't about to tell him she was and have
him spread the word around that she was . . . easy. She
had enough trouble with males without allowing any
gossips to talk about her. If her papa ever found out
she'd ever done anything so rash, he'd horsewhip Kyle.

She had used that very threat on occasion, and it
had had a sobering effect on most of the younger guys.
The older ones could handle being snubbed.

One guy had told her that she was completely
heartless. She'd just met him! So she'd said, "So are
you. Also your daddy didn't do much in raising you.
He should have given you more direction." His daddy
worked for her daddy.

Then she'd gotten out of his daddy's car and begun
to walk home. That had infuriated her date and he'd
had to drive in a crawl alongside her to see her the
three miles home.

He'd rolled down her car window and said, "Get in.
I won't touch you." And he'd said it in a deadly way.

She'd told him to go jump.

He'd snarled that she'd never marry.

And she'd replied, "Not you, anyway."

He'd married young and their first baby had arrived about six months later. He played a lot of golf,
and his wife stayed home with their kids. He was a
rotten father.

So she'd made a lucky escape on that one. And she
could remember some others. But she'd lost a couple
of really earnest guys who'd honestly wanted to
be . . . her daddy's son-in-law.

Several would have been charming husbands. They were courteous and attentive. But they'd mostly wanted to just be kin to her daddy.

And she tried to think of any of the courters who'd wanted . . . her.

Yeah. There'd been a couple. She just hadn't wanted them . . . enough.

Courtship and marriage were a nuisance. It was difficult and serious. And right over there, in the same room, was a tricky man who'd pretended to be a ranch hand, who'd admitted he'd been in her court at the Fiesta some years back.

She didn't remember him.

She wondered if he lied.

People do lie. If it will soothe someone or postpone something, people will tell something acceptable to the other person. Like her daddy telling her mother a super storm would be "all right" and they would be okay.

Her daddy hadn't had one clue that it was the Storm of the Century. But he'd lied and calmed her mother who in turn had calmed those there. Her mother had been serene and logical even as the roof of the house had been damaged and partially lost.

The lightning in the storm had been spectacular. The rain had blown so hard that it was parallel to the ground. Lauren had never seen anything to compare to it. It had been awesome. What had it looked like from space?

It had probably seemed local because it moved on up the East Coast in a remarkably short time. The rest of our planet was okay. It was a storm only in that portion of this earth. It was wicked. And her father had told her mother, "It's okay." And her mother had believed him.

Was her mother gullible?

Lauren wondered if perhaps she had gotten her genes from her mother? Had her mother been as literal as her second daughter? It was a curse.

And it was then that Lauren decided it was her own life. She should make her own rules. She was mature and in control. She could live her life as she damned well pleased.

That was a heady decision. She looked at Kyle differently. He watched her with avid eyes . . . and some caution.

She said, "The fire's nice. Thank you."

"You're welcome."

She smiled a little. "Which is my sofa?"

"That one's closer to the fire."

She tilted her head and considered. "You'll probably be so hot that you'll turn your sofa away from the fire."

"I'll turn it away from you." He meant she was the heat.

She didn't get it and said, "I knew it. You're probably like my daddy and rarely wear a coat."

"I'll bet you take after your mother."

"Actually, I've just begun to notice Mother and I are similar."

"In what way?" he asked, tilting his head back and watching her with avid interest from under his thick eyelashes.

"Just in little things." She shrugged. "I always thought I was like my daddy." She was busily arranging the pillows on the sofa and discarding some to one of the chairs. She was like a busy mouse who still didn't know a cat was watching.

She admitted, "I'm more like my mother."

"How?"

"Ah, I am almost as logical as my mother. My imagination isn't vivid. I have a level head."

In those silks, she leaned and moved and reached and about drove him crazy. She walked back and forth being neat and tidy, and the fire showed her silhouette.

How could she be so unconscious of herself and of her effect on him? He was trying to curb his reaction because she was obviously so unknowing. At her age? She had to still be under thirty. In fact, since she had been eighteen when she was Queen of the Fiesta, she had to be about . . . twenty-seven.

And if he was any judge, she was still a virgin. How could that be?

He'd bet on it.

That meant she never carried condoms and she didn't have a diaphragm. She probably never had. Well, it was going to be a test to be with her for three days in such close encounters.

The house was big. He could go to the barn. He'd bring the dog inside. He wondered if one of the barn cats would come inside the house.

With the milking of the cows, the cats and dogs came for the leftover milk. They didn't crouch or scatter when he was there. He might could get a cat inside.

Then after she left, how would he convince the cat or dog to stay outside?

His mother had told him, "Don't let them inside to begin with, and you won't have any trouble with the animals."

"Mice?" he'd asked nicely.

"Use traps." His mother had been logical.

He'd gasped in elaborated consternation and asked, "And open the traps to let the tiny little bodies drop into—"

"Hush!" His mother had speared him with wide, shocked eyes.

He'd laughed.

How like a man.

So with the evening quickly darkening and the winds shrill and buffeting against the house and carelessly waggling the trees, Kyle went out to the barn to see if any of the livestock—not cows, not horses...not inside—if some of the smaller animals wanted to go back to the house with him.

One dog was willing. The dogs were male and neutered.

The one cat that he could pick up was fat and had long fur. It hung on his arm like a rather ratty mottled neck fur from olden times.

Kyle carried the cat through the snow. They went into the house, and Lauren was in the kitchen. She turned and said, "Get that cat out of here!"

So he didn't even pause but swung around and vanished back through the door to the outside. He left the dog in the kitchen while he returned the cat to the barn. It didn't mind. The cat probably hadn't minded the trip.

When Kyle returned, he inquired with interest, "Why not the cat?"

Readily, she replied, "The cat's fur is the type that a victim of owning such a cat would require all the person's attention and innovativeness in trying to get the fur under control."

A simple response.

He squinted his eyes. "You're neat." A rather censoring statement.

With acceptance, she shrugged and replied the truth, "Relentlessly."

"My God. We'll be here a good three days. Try to control yourself."

"I decline doing attics or basements."

"Where did you ever find a basement down here?"

"My grandmother. They lived on a hill. Part of the structure was a basement."

"And she was neat?"

Lauren repeated the identity. "Overwhelmingly."

"I shudder to have you in my house."

"It's only for three days, and I am old enough to control myself."

"I'm just thankful for that."

She nodded soberly. "Count your blessings."

"I will. The entire time. If I look lax, mention just the word."

"Basement?" she inquired nicely.

"Neat," he corrected.

"I shall."

He watched her for a while before he admitted, "My mother would love you."

"She's neat?"

"She was so tacky and careless, she got out of any side of the bed that was handy. My daddy mentions that now and then."

"I'll bet she's a great cook."

He nodded. "And she can do any handwork you'd mention."

With some preening, Lauren threw in gently, "I can tat."

"Glory be."

And Lauren laughed. Her eyes sparkled and her dimples were deep. She had dimples.

"I haven't seen many blond women who had dimples and brown eyes."

"Don't be impressed. It's what's inside, and I'm a stickler."

Kyle's head nodded slowly. "Thanks for the warning."

"It saves time for a male to understand from the beginning."

He observed, "You play a mean game of cribbage."

"I'm good at poker, too."

"We'll go to Vegas while the storm's running, and I'll back you."

"With the snow, we'd be stuck in some awful place between here and there."

He looked confident. "I'd have coins, and we'd match for them."

"I'd win."

He considered her. "Yeah. You would."

She had the downstairs bathroom. He went upstairs. She was seemingly asleep on the sofa nearest the fire when he came back.

He saw that the lights were already dimmed. He lay on his back, watching the fire dance on the ceiling.

When the flame gentled, he put more dense wood on the fire. He went to sleep thinking what an odd day it had been. Then he thought of the day to come.

Lauren wakened to look around the different room. Where was she? She did recall and looked for him. He was gone.

Then she heard his footsteps on the back porch, and he came in with a dog.

They stood in the open sliding door entrance and looked at her lying on the couch. Neither male made a sound.

She said, "Good morning."

Kyle smiled, but he didn't reply. The dog moved but was again still. He was uncertain.

Kyle asked, "Want some coffee in bed?"

"No, thank you. I'll get up."

The two males left the door and their steps went to the kitchen.

After a time she managed to get up from the couch and go to wash her face in the downstairs bath.

She followed the aroma of the coffee to the kitchen. And she just sat down on one chair and ate what Kyle served.

She moved her head slowly and slightly as she looked around the room. "The house is well-done. Did you furnish it?"

"Most of the stuff was already here. My mother and sisters and both brothers put their oars in, giving advice and arguing and debating how it all should go."

"Who won?"

"They did. I ran some beeves up to the railroad spur for the market. Both brothers caught up with me and gave me—heck—for not telling them I was leaving."

"So your mother and sisters were here all alone, and they did the house to ease their boredom?"

He squinted a trifle as he almost shook his head. "I don't think they noticed we were gone."

Having finished breakfast, she said, "It is interesting. May I look around?"

And he replied, "Suit yourself."

Because the house was so cold, she wore his sheepskin coat.

Kyle trailed along. She examined rugs and turned the corners over to see if they were stamped. They were woven. And she tested the chairs and beds. She opened doors. They were the kind that were paneled like the old doors.

She asked Kyle, "Where did you get the doors?"

He gestured. "In San Antone, there're stores that've got all sorts of old things from old houses that've been razed."

"Your mother and sisters chose well."

He scoffed. "They're a nuisance."

She put out her hands, palms up. "And you just gave up and let them do as they wanted?"

He grinned as he nodded. "I like their houses. I don't find anything in this house that irritates me. They mostly replaced the window hangings. They had some lamps rewired. And they chose the wallpaper."

He looked at her as he said that and watched her reaction as she studied the paper in the hall. She said, "It's perfect."

He corrected, "It's old-fashioned."

But she told him, "For the way this house is arranged, it's perfect."

"I'll tell them I had just such a comment."

"You do, and they'll hound you until you tell them who I am, and then you'll go crazy with their questions."

"They know you?"

She was patient. "They'll wonder why you had a woman here."

He opened out his hands with logic. "I'll tell them about the storm."

"You idiot. You'll make them so curious!"

He chided her. "I've always been an honest man—"

"—until you play cards."

He took a patient breath. "I suppose I'll *never* hear the end of that one."

"You'll hear it only until I leave. After that, you'll be safe. I never gossip." But then she mentioned, "Of course, when I don't show up with the pod, some of the crew will come looking, and after a day or so, they'll come back to the drop, and they'll find my car. It's a convertible and the top was down. It'll be full of snow."

He disagreed. "Not with the gulf wind that'll be coming back along. That'll dry it out in no time."

Even the banisters along the back stairs had been denuded of paint and the oak was simply beautiful. Lauren ran her hand along the wood and she felt such pleasure. "The woods are so beautiful."

He was watching her pleasure in the grain so perfectly exposed. But he was watching her. And when she said the word "beautiful," he said, "Yes." But he was still looking at her.

She only questioned the drapes on the west in the bedroom upstairs.

He responded, "It's the evening sun. We have only new trees on this side, and you've got to know about summer sun?" The questioning statement. "So we've got thick, porous drapes which allow the breeze while it blocks the sun."

She nodded. "Smart."

"You should have listened to the harangue over it all. That's when I took the cattle for a walk."

"—to the railroad spur."

"Yeah. I didn't get as much for them that early, but I did get away from the donnybrook."

"Irish?"

"Yeah. Some. Why?"

"You called the confrontation a donnybrook."

"There's a real town by that name in Ireland. I went there." He grinned. "And I kissed the Blarney Stone. My grandfather was in Ireland long, long ago, as a very young man, and at that time he kissed a great, round stone that was on the ground. I went two years ago and they've moved the 'Blarney Stone' to the top floor of an old, roofless, stone castle and you pay to kiss what they now call a Blarney Stone. It's blarney, okay. One way or the other."

"You believe the Irish tease us?"

"More than likely."

And Lauren grinned. She didn't laugh out loud because she bit her lower lip and managed to control her humor. She said to her host, "You are an interesting person."

And he replied, "So are you."

Five

As they moved along in their tour of his house, Lauren regarded Kyle with some care. He was a man. Her eyes dipped down. Yes, indeed, he surely was a man. Like just about every other man, he was interested in women. She was a woman. There was one hell of a blustery storm outside. They were in the house together and no-body-else was any-where-around.

Of course, that was a sobering thought to a protected woman. It gave pause to a woman even twenty-seven years old. She was alone in a serious storm with a stranger who was definitely male.

She shivered. Well, it *was* cold in the house.

That shiver wasn't from cold. Her body smiled. Now, how could a body smile? It smiled.

Her brain said, *Yeah!*

But her conscience was still prim and prissy. That was a surprise. She'd never before realized her conscience was so strong. Really, it was rather adamant. How strange to understand she had no real control. It was as if she was a bystander listening to a debate argued by her staunch conscience.

Her brain smirked shockingly and said, *We'll just see how strong it is!*

Now what did *that* mean?

If the storm went on the predicted two more days, she just might find out.

After going along with the humans on their tour of the house, the dog felt quite at home. He was an alert, silent chunk of accommodation. If anyone wanted to do anything, it was okay by him. He was a watcher. Bored, he was interested in any kind of activity. So the dog had gone along on the tour. He'd been discreet, silent, tolerant and curious.

Kyle considered that the house was still shipshape. A strange word to use in the vast land space of cattle- and oil-ruled TEXAS. However, in olden times, cantankerous budding men or hard nosed, difficult ones were shipped off by their families out to sea for a year or so of limited activity. Ships tend to be an island on the sea. Kyle knew it well.

Such an isolation generally happened when the males were about twenty.

Budding women never had to be disciplined. Or maybe, the families just didn't trust defying women to get out from under the parents' thumbs?

At any rate, that young male sojourn in the Gulf allowed some iron-willed ship captain to teach the recalcitrant sons-of-friends some manners. Or at least they were taught to listen to and obey orders.

It was either be disciplined or the Captain mentioned hungry sharks. He never had to actually thrash a difficult sailor under his command. But his mate didn't mind doing it when his patience was spent. And there was the shark threat. Out on the sea, here and there, there *were* sharks.

Courtesy of his father, Kyle had had a year on the Gulf. His confrontation with reality was after he'd been back on the land. He was still lifting his face to the breezes and breathing the winds to tell which kind of clouds those were. It was almost seven years since his year long cruise after which he'd finished college.

That was when his parents had a special party, and one of the guests was... the ship's captain! Kyle was startled.

The slow-moving, calm, block of a seaman smiled and said, "Hi, sailor." He never remembered their names. Not those of the sons of his friends who had been sent to him on the sea. He'd harbored over twenty such problems by then.

That was when Kyle thought if ever a son of his was difficult, he would be sent to sea during his junior year. That was the year of revolt. That was the year when males particularly decided they needed to guide their own lives.

And that was why the U.S. services took recruits at eighteen. They still responded to directions at eighteen. By twenty, males wanted the control of their lives.

As the storm-trapped pair and the barn dog returned to the kitchen from their chilly venture through the house, Kyle asked Lauren, "Have you ever been to sea?"

"Only to fish in the Gulf. The boat was strange and had several decks. I thought it was top-heavy and dangerous. I wore a life jacket the entire time, carried a yellow flag and stayed on deck."

Kyle nodded. "I was in a ship once that had a hull leak. They had to have the pump going all the time. No one else seemed to worry about it."

"People are strange."

Kyle blinked a time or two as he looked at the woman in sand-colored silks who had been out on the land, alone, looking for a gourd-pod with a cloth tail. She thought other people were strange?

Her eyes were cast down as she watched the dog. She seemed unaware of Kyle Phillips. He tried to think of a time when he'd been with a young, unmarried woman who *hadn't* looked at him or been aware of him.

If there had been one, Kyle hadn't noticed her.

He noticed this one.

If the circumstances they were in now were in a book, she would look up and ask, "Your room or mine?"

Sure.

This one was a flag-waving holdout. She wasn't at all interested in a tangle with a stranger. She was of that ilk. If she ever gave in, it would be with gritted teeth and clenched fists, lying rigid on her side of the bed and being noble.

But as he thought that, her eyes slid up to him and she almost smiled as she blushed.

Kyle turned into vulnerable mush. And he had not one clue as to how to act or what to say to her. So he reached out his hand, palm up.

She hesitated, almost, then she put her cold small hand in his rough warm one. And he preceded her as they walked silently down the back stairs to the warm kitchen.

But he didn't want to let go of her hand. So he walked her over to the back door. They stood, looking out at the storm roaring recklessly, indifferent to all the storm-trapped creatures who survived...so far.

Oddly, their reactions were parallel. They didn't speak or even move, they were so delighted with what they saw. They were trapped there, together.

There was no way for anyone to come to them, or for them or even to contact them. They were Adam and Eve. Alone in the maelstrom of the beginnings of the world.

She asked gently, "How will you ever get to the barn for the cows?"

He grinned and sighed with great dramatic talent. "So you aren't going to volunteer?"

She laughed, "In these?"

And under her opening coat, he again saw those soft, sand-colored silks. His body almost went into overdrive at the very idea of what they covered. The silks weren't very subtle.

So he pushed his hands down into his pant pockets, and he said, "What sort of bribe do you need to slough your way out to the barn for the sake of other females in distress?"

She tilted her head as she raised her eyebrows a tad. She seriously considered the premise before she replied, "Nothing I can think of right now."

His eyes sparkled and he bit his grin. "Consider it. That's all I'll ask. I'll do the food and clean up and make the beds and feed the dog and let him out and wait for him, if you'll agree to go out there through that blizzard and milk the cows."

"What happens if the cows aren't milked?"

"They'll be very uncomfortable and miserable. They'll moo endlessly and make a racket. The milk will finally leak or clot and they won't give any more." That was approximate.

"I do know how to milk a cow. My grandmother saw to it."

"Your precious, fragile *grandmother* knows how to milk a cow?"

"She had a strident mother."

He licked his grin. "You strident?"

"I think I could grow into it... quite comfortably. I find other people aren't as skilled or knowledgeable as they seem. Incapable, they are simply ready to take over. I could do that."

And he cautioned, "Don't scare me."

She laughed. Her eyes sparkled and her teeth were white. She didn't smoke or chew or spit tobacco. She smelled like a woman. There was only her sweet essence. She didn't need to wear a covering scent.

He told her nicely, "I like the way you smell."

"Do gentlemen say that to ladies? I'm not wearing a perfume."

He shrugged as he communicated something obvious, "Some gentlemen say it."

Her head was down and she turned it a bit to look at him from the corners of her eyes. "Obviously, you are one who does that."

He licked his smile again. But his eye crinkles betrayed his humor. Women are just so different. He wanted this one. Would she be appalled? Would she think he was gross? An animal?

He studied her movements carefully. He saw that she didn't retreat from him. She stood her ground. He became aware of how she looked at him, and gradually, it came to him that if he was clever and smooth, she just might respond to his lusts. Yes!

He mentioned the storm to his guardian angel and congratulated him for contriving it so handily. In response, Kyle felt the guardian was bored, indifferent and rather killingly patient.

Well, Kyle was quite certain he could handle this episode by himself.

And as it does happen, Kyle's thoughts were very similar to the thoughts inside Lauren's head. And *her* guardian angel was over by the oven, bored out of her gourd and even less patient than Kyle's.

The dog didn't mind. He could smell the intense interest between the two humans. It was just amazing to the dog that the two humans took so long.

With interest, Lauren asked, "What is on the entertainment agenda?"

Kyle's ears perked up and his eyebrows lifted just a tad but his eyes danced with all sorts of lights. She found that fascinating.

He inquired, "More cribbage? Five-card stud? Dice a dollar a throw? Television?"

"How can the TV work without electricity?"

"Right. There's one of the old telescopic double-card viewers from long ago. Great three-dimensional visuals. See? There are all kinds of entertainment." And, yet again, he licked his smile.

She *was* twenty-seven. She knew he was being verbally clever, saying things that were salacious— Well, maybe he was a gentleman and was *not* salacious.

Maybe he meant exactly what he said, and it was only her own wild and wicked libido that was berserk.

How did one know?

She could ask him. *Are you being salacious?*

If she did, he'd probably not understand and be shocked by her assumption.

She was going to have to be clever and slow in order to lead him into allowing her access to his body.

That made her sound very like some disease. It was he who would do the invading.

Uh-huh.

Why was this time in her life suddenly so sexually greedy? Had such conduct been coming on in this last year? Was her restlessness and lack of direction a part of all this? Was it her body that was so rampantly hungry? She was rather shocked by her body's animal conduct.

But she looked at him. He was waiting for her to decide what she wanted to do in order to spend useless time while they waited for the storm to go on past them.

She told him with some interest, "When I was little, I thought first that the rain fell all over the earth at the same time."

He nodded in understanding.

"Then when it rained, and I saw rain in the distance and none where I was, I figured it rained there until the cloud was empty."

He understood that.

"Now the TV shows us that the storms gather in the Pacific and go across there and clear across our country—never faltering—and on out into the Atlantic. That is incredible."

"Yeah." He watched her with some attention.

"This storm." She gestured to the kitchen window. "It will go on up the East Coast and then into Canada or out into the Atlantic. Still being just the way it is now."

He wasn't especially fascinated but he was courteous. He gave her his attention and nodded.

She shared her observation: "The world is strange. How did we get here?"

"You were wandering around on the far side, and I took you up on my horse."

She looked up at him and smiled. "I thought you might be an illusion."

"Feel me." His voice turned foggy. "I promise you that I'm real."

With the invitation, she took advantage of the offer and she put her hand on his chest. She smiled into his hot eyes and said to him, "You're real."

He thought, *Now!*

She said, "Let's play cribbage." And she turned away from him to go over to the kitchen table.

The game was hell-bent and aggressive. Their cheerful competitiveness accelerated. They leaned forward, they watched the played cards avidly and they yelled! They whooped and hollered and they laughed. They sat back and just grinned at each other. It was great.

She said with curiosity, "Some people just play quietly and only occasionally make a sound. I've never played with such fun. Thank you."

Kyle gathered the cards to shuffle them and told Lauren, "If you weren't here, I'd be trying to train that dog to play cards. Look at his enthusiasm. Is he on that chair, watching, learning?"

The dog was asleep on an oval braided rug in front of the open door of the stove. The heat went up from him. He wasn't in the line of the heat pouring from the oven. Like all sedentary animals, he had gauged his nap place just right.

Their lunch was casual. She went through his refrigerator and found odd things. She would ask with interest, "What is this?"

He soothed in a wonderfully offhanded way, "It's only been there a while."

And she moved to pitch it.

"Hey! That's still good."

"Three days later? No."

And he was astonished. He protested with indignation, "It's good!"

"How much do you cherish the dog?"

"We have animal drop-offs as a continuing resource. People think farms and ranches need animals. That isn't true. A lot of the animals try to get back home and they die doing that. The others aren't as faithful. They're probably smarter. They come and go. That dog's been here about a year. He's sturdy. He can handle a three-day-old, refrigerated piece of meat."

Lauren made a face and pronounced the word precisely, "Yuck."

And Kyle proclaimed in some surprise, "You're just like my mother!"

"I doubt it."

He shook his head. "I mean your attitude. She's picky, too."

"She has excellent taste."

He grinned.

And Lauren explained drolly, "The skill I mentioned in your mother was in decorating a house."

"Her daughters helped. The arguments I had would wobble you."

And with curiosity, she asked, "What sort of things did you want that they canceled?"

He looked on her as if she'd turned into a conspirator. "The drapes, the rug on the stairs...I wanted the bare wood. The umbrella stand with all those weeds—"

She gasped in shock before she declared, "That umbrella stand with the perfect bouquet is outstanding!"

He mumbled, "The stand is outstanding?"

She was continuing, "The rug on the stairs will soften the steps of any wild and woolly kids you have here."

"I'm a bachelor."

She shook her head. "You'll get around to kids eventually."

He scowled at her. "I'll get around to having kids? I need a woman, first."

"Some strange female will come out here and love the blank countryside and will tolerate you in order to live in this perfectly furnished house. And she will happily give you children."

Not her? Is that what she was telling him? He'd have to find another lost woman and harbor her there until she gave in?

"I have a town house." Now why had he blurted that?

Lauren nodded thoughtfully. "That just possibly may save your wife's sanity."

He guessed, "You don't like the open land."

She considered and replied, "It's nice to look at it as you drive through it."

He'd run into that attitude before. Women tended to like cities. But there were some women who loved the countryside. He asked, "Do you know of any women who'd like living out here?"

She considered the premise thoughtfully. She regarded him as if she was wondering if any woman would have him. Then she said, "I'd have to research."

"The land?"

She looked at him. "Women."

"Oh." She would let go of him and just find him a woman? His ego was singed. So he said to her, "I have some specifications for any contender to the throne." He looked at Lauren.

"Throne? You think living here, for a woman, would be a superior opportunity?"

He had to shift his feet and considered his reply before he replied honestly. "Yeah."

She looked around at the house. "I suppose it would be—for some woman. The house is excellent. But there are no other women around in this area." She looked at him soberly. "Your wife would be lonely."

"You want me to have a harem?"

And he loved the indignation that shadowed her face so briefly.

She turned away as if considering. Then she said in an instructing manner, "A woman needs a shopping center nearby with a small grocery, a beauty parlor, a bank, a nice dress shop and a shoe store. It would be nice to have an ice cream parlor."

He took her arm and escorted her into another
room. There was another refrigerator and two deep
freezers. There were shelves and cupboards, which
were filled with canned goods, bags of beans and
boxes of cereals.

He answered her gently, "Y— She wouldn't starve."

"What about neighbors?"

So he took her to another room and to that window and gestured in directions. "Over thataway are
the Bigses. Down yonder are the Muellers, over there
are the Quills and in that direction are the Yarbor-
oughs and the Smiths."

"You have Smiths clear out here?"

He shrugged as he lifted out his hand. "There're
Smiths everywhere." He watched her, then he told her,
"Y— She'd have a car of her own."

She thought of her convertible filled with snow.
Soberly, she agreed, "Just having one would be a link
to civilization."

"You don't think this is a part of civilization?"

"Where?" She went to the window of that storage
room. Her arms were around her silk-clad, shivering
body.

He told her, "Everywhere. We have Rangers out
here, and we have Sheriffs and we have good neighbors."

"I'll see what I can do about finding you a wife."

"You're cold." He put his hand on her shoulder.

She turned up her face to see him. "I'm frozen."

He looked into her brown eyes and saw yellow
flecks. And he was so mesmerized that he didn't do the
logical thing and take her back into the kitchen. He
just looked down into her eyes.

He was so serious that his eye crinkles were white in his tanned face. He was stunned by her.

She shivered. And he took off his shirt and gave it to her. He was then in a T-shirt and twill trousers. He wore boots. His hands were warm on her cheeks.

His hands were on her cold cheeks. She was watching him as he came closer. And he kissed her. She was so startled that her lips parted with her surprise and she almost didn't get time enough to kiss him back.

So as he lifted his mouth from hers, her mouth followed his up. But in time he realized that and stopped and moved his head back down to really, really kiss her.

She was, by then, wrapped in his arms and against his nice warm body. She burrowed closer. Her wiggling to get closer was very stimulating for him. He said, "Let's go—"

And she interrupted, "I'm freezing and I need to get back into the kitchen."

"You're cold?" He looked astonished.

She said, "Yes!" being quite clear about it.

And he moved out a hand to indicate the door to the kitchen. But she was already through it, by the oven and holding herself as she shivered inside his warm shirt.

She closed her eyes, crossed her arms around the shirt and said, "Ummm."

She said that about his flannel shirt. He frowned. He could find another. Maybe the silks really were foolish. But he hated the idea of her putting on more clothes.

The dog had stood up with her intrusion into his space. Lauren was standing, bent to the stove with her hands in the rising heat. The dog stood blinking sleepily and watching the strange behavior of the two strange creatures who were back in the kitchen.

Kyle told her earnestly, "We never have ever had any outages here."

She slowly, unbelievingly slid her eyes over to his in dismissive disbelief.

Gloomily he promised, "I'll find you some heavier clothes."

She didn't reply, and he went off out of the kitchen. Then he remembered to come back and close the door to the rest of the house. She listened; his steps went on-off and the sounds of him disappeared.

That way, Lauren had a brief taste of what it must be like to be alone. Kyle had lived there in that big house, all alone, for some time. That must explain why he was so concentrated on her. She was female. She was there. He had just kissed her.

Also, there was this mammoth storm. The electricity was out. She was all the entertainment Kyle had. Since she could speak in words, she probably even beat out the dog as a companion.

Hmmmm.

She would have to protect Kyle from himself. With this chatter about what a cozy place it was, there, he could well propose to her. He could get that done before the storm was past and he could get out again.

It would be good exercise for him to go out and milk the cows. How many did he have? She could help him with that. It had been years since she'd done it. But it was probably like crocheting. One never forgets an acquired skill.

And she remembered her mother trying to figure out her sewing machine after years of not using it. At one time, her mother had made all of the daughters' clothing.

Her mother's sewing had gone on until the daughters' rebellion in ninth grade. Each had wanted to look like everyone else.

Females aren't as weird as males.

Kyle returned to the kitchen with some cedar chest treasures of woolen ski clothes. "These belonged to one of my sisters. Try them." He said it sadly as he took a last lingering study of the silks.

"I can't wear wool." She was equally sad as she said that.

But he brightened and smiled. "I'll see if I can find something else. And he cheerfully went back upstairs.

She found herself wondering, what was a bachelor doing with a cedar chest of women's clothing? And she waited for his return.

He did come back. And he carried some odd assortments of wear that were not at all coordinated. But they were fascinating.

She tried on everything. Most were too small. Had he been deliberate? She felt like a whale.

He sat at the kitchen table and watched her try things on over the silks. He liked the silks. If he agreed to marry her, would she wear only silks? Or nothing? He told her, "The heat will be on soon. We have a good crew."

She replied seriously, "I need to find something else to wear because these silks need to be washed."

He replied "I have a good washer and dryer in the washroom. It's over here." He went and opened another door.

She hadn't seen it on their tour of his house. She asked, "Have you anything you would like to have washed?"

He replied gently as he watched her seriously, "We'll have to wait for the electricity to come back on."

And she was stopped. She stood and considered. Then she said, "Yes."

He immediately went into a long dissertation on how seldom the electricity was off. It was trustworthy. It was there. This was an unusual storm. They had *always* had electricity.

She listened, sober faced, and when he was repeating things, she nodded—once.

A woman nodding once was not communicating a full hearted agreement.

Six

_____

The gathering of clothing, which he'd found, was not good. She looked at his own clothing. "Let me check out your closet."

He was taller than she; he was heavier in weight by about fifty pounds. His clothing would not fit her. To prove that he was a caring male, he said to her kindly, "We could look."

She got the sheepskin coat and put it on. They went upstairs to his room. He especially liked seeing her in his room. Even in the coat, he liked her in his room. How could he get her into his bed?

She opened his closet and looked at the shirts. She asked carefully, not looking at him, "Who irons your shirts?"

"The laundry does it. They even pick them up and deliver them. Naw. I was kidding. I take whatever it is there every week and pick it up in a couple-a days."

She looked at the shirts more carefully. "They do a good job. How much do they charge?"

"Oh, around a buck each."

"That isn't bad. They appear to do a good job. I believe I'll wear this corduroy one."

Openly, he exclaimed, "You can have it! It's too hot for me."

"Thank you."

His breathing changed. While his breaths were high in his chest, he carefully asked, "That all? You just gonna wear the shirt?"

Busily going through his clothes, she replied, "No. I'll find some trousers and some heavy, cotton socks."

He was sunk. She'd be covered from her nose to toes. Damn. But he said, "I can find the socks. And here's some cords that'll be okay. With a belt. Naw. You'll need a tie to hold them up. Let's see. Here's— Uh, not that one. This— Naw. Maybe this—"

He was fond of his ties and wanted them treated well, not tied around some female waist to hold up pants. In the back of the closet, there it was, a tie from his grandmother. "Here's one."

She accepted it with only one blink to reveal her surprise. "Where did you find this one?"

"My grandmother who is color blind. You don't *ever* tell her."

His grandmother. That would explain it. She smiled at him.

Then he handed the cords over to her as if they were precious. "I haven't worn these in a while. They're clean. You can try them."

And he waited.

She looked at him and said, "I'll take a rinse off and wash my silks. The bathroom will be heated by the water."

He watched her soberly for a minute before he admitted, "The water's heated by electricity."

"No...hot...water." It wasn't a question. It was a defeated statement.

"I can get you some hot water on the stove?" The TEXAS questioning statement. "I'll pour it into the bathtub downstairs. Okay? I'll go get it started." And he immediately turned away to do it.

She could handle that. She called after him, "Thanks."

The words came back. "I'm your host."

His mother had always managed to mention that he should never pick up stray females.

"—unless they're beeves," his dad would add on.

So there Kyle Phillips was, out in the middle of nowhere on his own place, with a stray woman in his house. He smiled. She sure was something!

With her vividly in his excited mind, Kyle filled two buckets and a kettle. That ought to be enough water for a woman's bath. With all the physical work he did, he very easily set the filled buckets on the stovetop and turned on the gas.

Watched pots never boil. He went back up the stairs, and she was still in the sheepskin coat and she'd laid out what she wanted.

Why would she wear all that stuff?

And he considered that if she was at all kind, she would invite him to bathe her. Yeah. He breathed and discarded the multiplication tables because he would rather hurt. The need was distracting. Now how could such discomfort be distracting?

It showed him what he didn't have.

He knew. He knew.

In the kitchen, Kyle finally could take some hot pads and carry the buckets to the downstairs bath.

Lauren had put some water into the tub so that the boiling water wouldn't hurt the tub. He poured in the hot water and asked, "Need your back scrubbed?" And he smiled in a sassy manner.

She shook her head, but she couldn't hide a little wicked smile of her own.

He had his hand on the doorknob. "If you don't add any water and you leave this door closed, the heat of the water will warm the room. I'll bring in more hot water for the bath."

"Thank you." She waited, and he watched her. He was silent, so she reminded him, "The other water."

"Yeah." But he still stood there, watching her. Finally, he turned the knob and slid out the door, rattling the buckets.

She closed the door.

He stood and his imagination saw her taking off those silks. Hell, she wouldn't do that yet. She'd let the room warm up first. Then she'd slide out of that soft material and her body would be naked. She'd smile at him, and he'd take her to bed. And he'd be so quick he'd be done and asleep before she'd even taken a breath.

He went back to the kitchen, refilled the containers and put them on the stove. It took a while for them to boil.

He paced. He wanted to go back to see what she was doing in that room. His imagination supplied the answer. She was stark, staring naked and waiting for him. Of course.

And he noted yet again that the gourd-pod for which she'd risked her life was lying on the breakfast table there in the kitchen. What was in it? What was put in a pod that was retrieved at risk of her very life? What could be that important?

Why would Lauren's bunch want to learn to deliver pods for information? What was written in the pod? Why was that bunch doing those tests? What was their purpose?

Eventually, the water boiled. He was eager and imagined her rising from the scant but cooled tub water like Venus on a half shell. Would she move her hands to cover herself?

He carried both buckets down the hall and tapped on the door with one boot toe.

She opened the door and was completely dressed in his sheepskin coat. It was hot and humid in the room. She closed the door after him, and he poured the boiling water into the tub.

He told her, "I have the kettle on the stove. I'll bring it right in."

"I probably don't need it. This is just great. Thank you."

And it was then that he saw she'd washed the silks. They were on hangers. They looked really fragile. If they were on the hanger, she was naked under his coat. The damned lucky, stupid, unknowing, unappreciating coat.

She said another, "Thank you," as she waited for him to leave.

He left, closing the door with some distracted care. He wondered if there were any spy holes in the house? He'd never thought to investigate such a thing. If there were, he would cover them. Of course. He would cover them . . . with his wicked eyes!

He went into the darkened closet next to the bath and closed the door. There wasn't one slit of light. Not even a skinny, little one.

How uninventive the previous owners had been. How dull their minds. They probably just went ahead and the woman had been willing so there was never any anticipation.

He was anticipating? Yeah. And he leaned back his head and silently groaned. Men had it tough. Women were stingy. They were fascinating. They ruled.

As silently as possible, he left the closet and went to the cooler living room. The kitchen was a furnace, what with the oven and the boiling water. The dog didn't mind.

Kyle narrowed his eyes as he observed the animal. That dog was a fooler. It had claimed to be a good, honest, cow dog. It had worked the beeves and been eager to make a good impression. But look what a basic house dog he was.

Kyle looked at the dog and told him with narrowed eyes, "You're a fooler."

And the dog laughed soundlessly. His panting was enough.

And Kyle retorted, "I am not, either!"

But the dog only smiled.

So Kyle warned, "Don't you dare tell."

The dog had to move, to walk with his nose down as he grinned even wider. How rude of such a dumb creature. Thank God the damned dog couldn't talk.

Meanwhile, in the bath, Lauren was sighing with exquisite pleasure to be that warm again . . . to be that clean. Her poor silks had been so dirty. The only thing that was good about that particular sparse TEXAS dirt was that it was mostly sand. It was just about the color of the silks and therefore the dirt hadn't been so obvious.

Finally, reluctantly, Lauren rose from the bath about like Kyle's imagination, Venus on the half shell. She dried with a skinny tufted towel. It was rather harsh. And she looked at his clothes.

She put them on.

How odd to feel invaded by him when she was wearing his clothing. Since she had no clean underwear, and he had provided none, his masculine clothing was against her soft, vulnerable body.

She paused to consider that feeling. How would it be to have his work-roughened hands on her, covering her? With his body?

She took deep breaths and her eyes closed. Her mind mentioned with some boredom that virgins were like that.

There wasn't anything happening to distract her from herself and what she wanted. Being isolated fooled virgins' minds into being crass. Away from civilization, the mind became basic?

She looked around the finely appointed room. This was basic? Not bad!

Kyle tapped on the door.

She had locked it. She asked, "Yes?"

And his husky, door-filtered voice said, "Don't empty the water, I'll bathe in what's there."

She looked at the almost clear water. He would bathe in the water—after her? Oddly hot licks writhed in her lower stomach. Places tightened, and some became lax. Her breasts got pushy.

All that with just the idea of him bathing in her bathwater?

The tub and the water were his; she'd only sat in it and bathed.

But *he* was going to bathe in it . . . now?

She suggested, "It's cooled."

Through the door, he replied immediately, "It's warmer than the snow outside."

That was, of course, true. She looked at herself in the mirror, and she was standing in his clothing. She was very covered. She'd never been so anonymous looking in all her born days.

If Kyle was to bathe, she ought to let him have the bath while it was still warm. She opened the door.

His eyes' sun wrinkles were pale as he looked at her avidly. She was wearing his clothes. It was his clothes that were hiding her soft body. His lips parted and he breathed rather erratically.

That happens when a couple find themselves snow-bound and the outside world doesn't seem real to them. They are isolated from the Universe. It's the Adam and Eve syndrome. Lauren understood that.

She left the bathroom quickly so that no more of the air would escape...or that none of the chilled air could get into the warm room.

Kyle watched after her with an abandoned look. She had left him there and escaped.

He saw her go back to the kitchen. She was really a weather sissy. No sense of raw adventure.

He closed the door after him and was socked by the heat. He took off his shirt and long-underwear top without any trouble at all. Getting his pants unzipped was a little more difficult. His long winter drawers were next.

His sex was urgent. Poor thing. There was nothing to satisfy it immediately. He undid his boots and peeled off his socks without any problem.

His sex was very alert. He sunk it into the still-warm water—where she had been naked. She had sat in that very place, stark naked. Realizing such a thing was no help at all for his libido.

He got clean. He emptied the tub and washed it out neatly. He had no clean clothes there. He considered all that as he toweled his body dry.

So he dropped his clothes in the hall and took the stairs two at a time to the landing. He looked back. She was nowhere around.

Why the disappointment?

He walked up the rest of the stairs and finally into his room. The cold didn't bother him. He left off the long john underwear and pulled on a shirt and jeans, socks and boots.

Naturally, he wore boots. He did it automatically. Any cattleman did. It was a lot like wearing a watch or carrying a gun. Boots were just a part of his life.

Kyle realized immediately that he should also turn off the gas on the stove. She needed to be cold enough to depend on heat—from him. He could manage some heat. Yeah.

And what would he do when he was lax and contented? She'd still be squirming all over him trying to get closer and warmer.

Okay.

He could handle that.

He brushed his hair, and he got his electric razor— No electricity. He'd turned it off to fake the storm was even worse than it was.

So he went back down to the bathroom. The water was drained out and gone. Since he was the one who'd cleaned out the tub, he should have remembered doing it. So he shaved in cold water.

It took a while to get his beard wet enough. Then the shaving cream did a pretty good job of it. And the razor was sharp. He did get it done. He rinsed his face and felt it with searching fingers. Not bad. He only had to add soap to about five places right around his mouth.

Lauren would need to know he'd shaved just for her.

Foolish man. Most beards and unshaven faces are exciting to a woman. It is just so different. The touch of the obviously male beard thrills her hands and her skin no matter where.

Well, rough faces were exciting to—most women. There were those who rejected beards. Foolish women.

And there Kyle was, clean and peeled like a newborn's backside.

Maybe he ought to have asked her if she was taken by a raspy-faced man?

What if she'd asked, "Who?"

So Kyle was uncertain when he went back into the last of the kitchen's warmth. After he fixed the gas line, only the living room's fireplace would give them heat.

Reality intruded and Kyle decided he'd cook some things first.

He found a nice small roast, some sweet potatoes, a quiche, and a frozen pie a woman had left for him. He put the pie and roast into the oven. Then he set the timer to remove the pie and put in the quiche and the sweet potatoes. That way the pie would be cooled just right by the time they ate.

Lauren watched Kyle with active interest but with no offer of help. She observed his diligence. She considered his menu. She was amused inside her head and body without showing any of it, and she was entertained.

At home, her father never lifted a domestic finger. Lauren had heard men were capable of caring for themselves but her father had given no indication such could be so.

Kyle was positive, efficient and practiced. He knew what he was doing. And it was done.

The two storm victims played cards, there in the warm kitchen. He watched his guest from under half-closed lashes. She still had some relaxed, warm time left. He wouldn't alter the gas line until the food was safely cooked.

He felt clever. He was amused at himself. He thought no other man in the world had ever pulled this trick on an innocent woman. Well, maybe. One or two other males might be as sneaky? It was remotely possible. He was secure that he was being innovative.

His smile should have tipped her off. His eyes danced with lights of amusement, and he felt so clever that he was a little animated.

Animated men are never up to anything good. It's a sign of underhandedness. Any moxie woman knows that. Since there was no flirting, or other woman around, his plans must be for her.

Lauren watched Kyle's conduct with interest. She suspected he was up to something. And she decided she'd go along with it—as long as it pleased her.

It was then that she realized just having him around pleased her. Why him? She looked at Kyle Phillips and considered him. He just might do for the long haul. How could that be? Just because he'd saved her from freezing?

How could she decide he was perfect on such a short acquaintance? Good gravy! She'd only met him yesterday. It was the storm. That's what had happened. She was lost out on that plain, but she hadn't yet admitted that she was lost. And he showed up like a magically conjured phantom.

It was the isolation. Him Adam. Her Eve.

Across the kitchen table, she observed him. He was a man. Not only was he attractively male, but he was an interesting person. He didn't brag. He liked her. He knew her from another time.

Of course, his admitting that had delayed her seduction of him. He was what? About thirty?

She asked, "Do you have any wife or kids, or an ex-wife?"

"No." He looked at her. "Neither do you have anybody like that."

"How much do you know about me?"

"You're not a display woman. You hated being Queen of the Fiesta."

She lifted her eyebrows in question. "That gives me Brownie points?"

"I'd not like—being around a woman who is part peacock."

"That's male."

He turned out his open palm. "—the female version."

"What do you look for in a woman?"

He smiled.

Disgruntled, the seducer-woman replied, "Men are so basic."

Gently, with a foggy voice lightened, he told her, "You would make any man a good mate. Besides not wanting to show off, you're independent, a little weird and you adjust to circumstances without complaining."

"My parents nailed our palms to the wall when we whined."

Knowing full well that wasn't so, he nodded. "Did it stop you?"

She responded, "We learned to debate." Then she added modestly, "I won a state championship." She looked up at him to see his reaction. She *was* a show-off if it was mental or skill. She didn't want to be window dressing or just know how to smile and wave.

He was interested. "You won the state contest?"

"Yes," she replied. Then she added, "But I lost to some bug-eyed male in D.C."

He inquired, "What was your subject?"

"Television versus computers for sports."

And he was curious, "Which side did you take?"

"Television. We have one that is the biggest tube viewing instead of a larger camera screen. I dislike sitting at a computer to watch TV."

"I have a computer."

"Do you use it?"

He shifted and put his arm over the back of his chair as he was deliberately smug. He told her, "I was one of the first to get an Apple II Plus. I still have friends from those first remarkable years. They were all smarter than me, and they were patient and led me along."

"Do you still have it?"

He was disgruntled. "The recently updated one is my seventh. It's flawed. It doesn't have sex or cook or make my bed."

She *tsked* once and shook her head. "How irritating."

He laughed and looked at her differently. He had expected her to either blush or be shocked or impatient or disgusted with him. She had responded perfectly. Now all she had to do was say that while she wasn't a computer, she could do all those other things.

She asked, "Who made the pie?"

It was cooling on the counter.

He seriously considered lying and saying it was his mother, but he told her honestly, "It's from one of the ladies who wants me to admire her cooking."

"Does she have . . . other talents?"

"I haven't asked." But then he watched her with such a slight, amused smile.

She admitted with some challenge, "I can't cook."

"I can."

"How did you learn? On the computer?" She was being rather snide.

"Mostly, I learned because I wasn't at home but was living alone. Peanut butter is a godsend, but there comes a time when other foods sound good. I began to cook. I'm not bad." He raised his eyebrows and tilted his head back to look at her rather sassily.

She responded with some earnest control, "That pie is driving me crazy." She was not competitive.

He grinned smugly and told her, "Actually, while it's not one I made, it's close to perfect. I'm sure about that, but I'll test it when it quits bubbling. It's too hot right now."

So she suggested, "Put it out on the back porch and get it cooled."

"You're hungry?" He guessed that with a complacent smile.

"I shouldn't be, but that aroma is driving me crazy!"

And he laughed. "Good!"

So he did get up and went to the counter where the alluring pie sat. He took some hot pads and lifted the pie. He asked with raised eyebrows, "Can you get the door? Open it when I get there and close it until I want back in, okay?"

She rose from her chair. She assured him with kind earnestness, "You can count on my not locking the door against you as long as the pie is out there, too."

He considered her with a pursed mouth. "You're how old?"

"Twenty-seven."

He exclaimed in shock, "If you are this ravenous at that young age, think how fat you'll be at forty!" And he shook his head and *tsked* his tongue.

She dismissed the premise. "You won't have to worry about it. I'll be long gone, and back under Goldilocks' rule."

He considered her words then questioned haltingly, "Goldilocks and the three bears?"

Lauren explained, "She's our cook. She's why I don't cook. Who could compete with her?"

He stood there by the counter and inquired, "She doesn't let you try to cook?"

Lauren shook her head in resignation. "Who can match her?"

He said earnestly, "You seem to be such a competitive woman. I'm surprised you haven't gone through cooking on your own."

"She doesn't let us in the kitchen," she exclaimed, putting out her hands in gestures. Then she added, "The only time she lets us in there is if we're clearing the table or sweeping the floor."

Kyle gasped. "How do you tolerate such a dictatorial person?"

"We love her." Lauren sighed in helplessness. "And she's the best cook in the whole country. We try not to let other people realize that. Daddy already pays her way beyond any logic."

Kyle considered as he licked his lips to stop the mental drool. "Would she come out and visit us?"

"Tomorrow?" Lauren frowned at Kyle.

"After we're married, wouldn't she worry about—"

"Married!"

"Well, yes," he replied with some resignation. "I've already given up on it. I realize that your daddy will demand I make an honest woman out of you. You'll be trapped here for three whole days, with just the two of us and with nobody else anywhere around. The dog's no chaperone at all. Your reputation will be shot all to hell. Everybody will whisper about you, but they'll slap me on the back and call me a clever sly coyote."

He explained kindly as he replaced the pie on the counter, "If people find you've been out here with me for three days, they'll realize you're compromised, and that I'm just sly. I'm not, of course. I'm an honorable man."

And she said, "Well, darn."

He was so startled that his sun wrinkles went white. He stared at her and his breaths were uneven and rather loud. Softly, he inquired carefully, "Darn?"

"I really thought I just might get you. I hadn't realized you are that honorable."

He stared.

She shrugged. "I'll have to go around denying everything. Just watch. No one will believe me. They'll nod and cross looks and they'll say sly things about us."

"If...if...if we *did,* what would you do when they taunted you?"

"Blush?"

And he began to smile. "Let me kiss you."

"If I get up out of this chair and come over to you, you'll claim I attacked you. My reputation will be ruined forever."

He considered her seriously. Then he mentioned, "If I come over there and help you stand up, will that, uh, balance the situation?"

She was earnest. "I wouldn't look quite so wicked."

Seriously, he asked, "But then, won't I look—forward?"

So she burst out laughing.

He shook his head and finally he grinned. "You are a surprise."

"Actually, you aren't surprised. You just don't know what to do about me."

He watched her avidly. Then he admitted, "Well...not yet...anyway."

So she inquired, "Are you going to take the pie out on the back porch?"

He looked at her soberly, then he looked at the pie. He looked back at her. "I don't think it needs to be chilled."

"So I don't get any now?"

And he told her seriously, "Maybe I can think of some kind of a distraction."

Her smile was slow and wicked.

Seven

Kyle didn't just walk over and drag Lauren off that chair. He grinned at her first, watching her, anticipating her willingness. Would she be willing?

He asked, "You've really—never—?"

"Not yet." But then she looked at him. Her eyes were like a deer's at night looking at the headlights of a car. She asked, "How many women have you tampered with?"

He gasped and put a hand on his hard chest. "Am I supposed to know what to do?" He protested, "I've never been in this here fix before, if that's what you're expecting. If I come over there and pull you out of that chair, what happens after I kiss you?"

She laughed.

His grin was perfect. He strolled across the floor. That was exactly what he did. He strolled over there in a cocky, male-dominant way that was perfect. He acted like he knew just *exactly* what he was doing, what he was going to do and what he'd do with and to her.

That gave her some confidence. She knew she had no idea at all how to go about this kind of sex thing. She shivered with nerves, with only a scant feeling of delight. She was excited and a tad scared at the same time. She felt rather recklessly rash. She asked, "Do you have any condoms?"

He hesitated just a tad before he told her, "I'll see if there're any in the house."

A little shocked, she inquired carefully, "You don't *know?*"

Quite smoothly with just the right pause, he told her, "Some couples have bunked here." He gestured. "They could have left some—unused ones." He bit his lips, but his eyes were so amused. "I'll check it out." Then he inquired, "Should I do that before I hype you up with one of my mind-boggling kisses?" He frowned at her. "Do you need all your brain cells functioning at one time?"

She loved it. "Let's go look for the condoms and be sure."

So he asked with interest, "Do you know what a condom looks like?"

"I've known a couple of females who carried condoms—just in case."

And he asked in shock, "And you don't do that?"

"I've never had any reason to do that, but now I wish I had. I certainly will after this."

"After...this?" He began to smile. "We'll see what's available. Want my coat?"

"Yes."

She was shivering with anticipation, but he thought she was cold and scared. He was especially gentle with her. He held the coat for her arms.

She turned to him very seriously and said, "I thought you were going to kiss me."

"I'll have to see if there're any condoms. I don't want to hype you up to screeching—*gasp*—and clawing—*gasp*—at my body—*gasp*—if there aren't any around."

With some obvious patience, Lauren said, "I wouldn't do that."

He was rather more surprised than men are ordinarily as he asked with great innocence, "I shouldn't look around?"

With patient calm, she supplied, "I wouldn't screech or claw at you."

He drew a deep breath as if he hadn't been breathing at all and he said, "I'm relieved. I thought my body was in danger."

"Good grief."

And he laughed. It was such a humorous, pleased, sharing laugh.

She sighed quite dramatically and gave him a patient look, but she had already begun to smile at him and that ruined her chiding look altogether.

So they went on the treasure hunt. He said, "I hope we find something. How vulnerable are you at this time of the month?"

"Very."

"Uh-oh. We'll have to hunt. I'm not giving out any free samples. Keep your distance."

She protested with some indignation, "I haven't touched you—as yet."

"Yeah," he scoffed. Then he asked, "Did you hear that 'as yet' you just said? You wicked woman! My daddy told me about women like you. I just hope you don't ravish me raw!"

Her laughter bubbled. She did try to smother it, but it just went on.

So he kissed her again. It was wonderful. It was amazing. It was wild sex and flaming loving. It was *great!* Then he finally, slowly lifted his mouth from hers with all those squishy sounds, and she panted. She did!

She moved her restless hands on his shoulders. She breathed and pressed her body against his. She couldn't keep her eyelids all the way open and her nose didn't work at all well. It was just a good thing her mouth knew how to take over and give her an input of oxygen.

But she didn't know how to go on. She didn't know to press or rub or move her hands. She didn't know what to say or how to act at all. She could barely control the fact that she was sexually wild and body hungry.

He hugged her to him with severely controlled, crushing arms and rigid, greedy hands. He laughed in his throat in such a wicked, wicked way. He said, "This is like a scavenger hunt. We've got to find a couple of condoms."

She managed to inquire, "A . . . couple?"

"Once won't be enough."

Wow! That was inside her head. *Wowwowwowwow!* A continuous celebration. But they did need a condom. At *least* one. She made her eyes open a little as her hands moved in his hair, and she asked, "Where all do we have to look?"

And Kyle replied with what should have been obvious. "All the bedside table drawers?"

She said, "Help me with the stairs."

It was only then that he realized she was exquisitely susceptible to him. To understand that it was true was so thrilling to him that he was close to being paralyzed right along with her.

So he scooped her up into his arms and the halt helped the lame in yet another incident. They made it up the stairs, into the first bedroom. And their search began.

There were seven bedrooms. That seemed a little rash. She asked, "Who all lives here?"

So as they searched the drawers, Kyle told Lauren, "Long ago, the people who owned this house, before the guy I bought it from, had twelve kids. Six were their own and then there were another six they took in."

"Wow."

He scoffed. "They probably worked those kids to a standstill."

"Do you really think so?"

Kyle was honest. "I have no idea. How're you doing? Can I put you back on your feet?"

"I like you carrying me."

He staggered with some skill. "Thank God you didn't have that pie."

She hastened to assure him, "I wasn't going to eat the whole thing."

"That's a relief."

So she said, "You can put me down."

He leaned his head down and kissed her very nicely. His voice was a little hoarse from emotion as he said, "I find I like carrying you."

"This is nice."

His husky voice said, "I know something that feels even nicer."

"I can't imagine what that could be."

"Me in you."

That jolted her. It was so explicit. It was so—crass. She gasped. And it was then that she became vividly aware of her body's independent response to his words. How shockingly basic was her own body! Who would ever believe that was so? And her eyes closed lazily as she smiled.

His laugh then in his throat was worse, better, wicked.

She chided, "Behave."

"I thought you wanted me to—"

"Hush!"

"You don't?"

"*Yeeessssss!*"

So she got kissed again. She didn't notice where they were or what bed he laid her on. She was so involved with just the sensations. Her greedy body was outrageous!

She felt him move her clothing aside and his kisses were distracting. She gasped and cooperated and wiggled to get closer and was involved!

He said, "Slow down." He said, "You wild woman!" He said, "Wow!" He said, "Honey—"

She was trying to pull him to her when he said, "Hold it! We need to get on the condom!"

She stopped, frozen, and her eyes opened. She said, "Hurry!"

He laughed helplessly. "You're a naughty woman!"

But his voice was soft and his chuckle was wicked.

He opened the drawer by the bed and exclaimed rather theatrically, "Here's a whole batch!" Then he looked at her like he'd spilled the beans. But he fooled her. He said, "I shouldn't have told you. Now you'll want to use them all!"

She smiled like Alice's Cheshire Cat and her eyes became wickedly sloe-eyed.

He was charmed. He'd heard of women like her but he'd never come across one. He'd had a couple. The women had been serious or woodenly enduring. He'd never encountered a one who was eager, sassy and fun. Of course, there'd been Billie Mae—but she'd just used him. Then she'd lain back and smoked a cigarette. It should have been a cigar.

Even Kyle's mind called it *cee*gar.

Lauren shivered. "It's so cold up here!"

And he said, "Move over so I can get in."

She moved over out of her warming spot, but then she shuddered and moved back.

He asked, "You after me?"

"I want my side of the bed back. You just put me there to warm it for you! You go on around to the other side."

"How could you be cold when you're under those blankets and still wearing my coat?"

"I'm fragile."

He nodded a couple of times like one of those fake birds that sit on the side of a whiskey glass. He said, "It's awful cold in here. Let's get friendly."

"My feet are freezing."

"So long as the rest's okay, don't worry about your feet."

He began stripping off all of his clothing! She was simply amazed he would be that bold. Her eyes got bigger.

He said, "I'm no threat. It's too cold."

His wallet fell out of his discarding pants. He told her, "Uh-oh. I *told* you it was cold. It just fell off."

She gasped.

He lifted the covers on the other side of the bed and slid in. He assured her, "I'm harmless. Be kind and warm me up."

And she said, "Maybe we can glue it back on. I saw a foreign glue commercial—"

He smothered his laughter in such amused chuckles as he gathered her close to him. "It's worth the try." But he added sadly, "It's frozen!"

"Maybe I can help."

She moved over on top of him.

From under her, he asked with some interest, "What are you doing?"

"I'm trying to warm your feet."

And he suggested kindly, "Let's work on what's important."

But she suddenly said, "You're not at all cold! You're hot!"

Then she gasped and repeated the words, "You're *hot!*" And she was amazed. "It's standing up straight." And then she asked, "Why's it wet?"

And he replied in the TEXAS questioning statement, "It's sweating? It's defrosting?" And with awe he told her, "You got the ice *melting!*"

She considered him in a still way before she accused, "You're a—sham!"

But he was earnest. He replied with such candor, "I'm an honest country boy. You're from the big city. You know what all there is to know. Teach me."

She took a deep breath and asked, "Has this approach ever been successful?"

"I'll let you know."

His sex thumped her stomach and she exclaimed, "It's alive!"

"Glory be! You saved it! I'm forever in your debt." He spread out his arms under the covers and moved his legs so that he was a large X. He told her, "Use me as you will. I'm your slave. Thank you."

Was she then an earnest seducer? No, she laughed. She giggled and lifted her head to look down at him. And she went on laughing.

One thing about virgins, they are always surprised by any ploy, and all the jokes are new.

So he got serious. He told her, "You are so magical. I saw you walking on my land in those silks, and I just wondered if you were real or some unreal storm siren sent by the winds to tempt me."

She sassed back, "I'm a vixen. A fox. I take strangers into my lure. You only think you're back home. You're actually in my lair and frozen. I'm using you."

He gasped in ham bone shock before he replied bravely, "Go ahead. I'll be brave."

So she ran her hand over his face and down his bare shoulders. She slid from him so that her leg was over his thighs and her hand was free to investigate and relish the pattern of hair on his chest, his stomach and around his excited sex.

While he was still and breathing shallowly and waiting, his sex was very interested and somewhat of a show-off.

"Hold it still."

"It has a whole life of its own. I'm only the keeper. It never pays me no never mind. I just do as told."

She asked, "It told you to seduce me?"

"It's very interested in you, sexually. The rest of me sees you as a human woman who is beautiful and sweet. It's a separate thing. I can't control Homer at all."

"Homer?"

"That's my sex. He acts out of all courtesy. He's forward and—a—homer. He wants inside you. It would be okay. He's got a sheath I put on him for you."

"I'm a little uncertain."

"You need coaxing? I thought if I would lie here quietly, you'd just go ahead and ravish me. What's holding you up?"

"I think it could be...reality?"

He gasped in shock before he scolded gently, "When Homer and I are so friendly and all? How could you be shy? You can surely tell Homer is willing. What on earth is making you hesitate now?"

When she didn't instantly reply, he went on, "You need to be kissed and reassured. Lie back on my chest. I'm warm. Your chest is chilled. Come here and let me help you get hot."

And he was certainly hot. As he kissed her and tried to figure out where to put his hands, his heat spread to her and the coat was too much.

When she began to struggle to get out of it, he became alarmed. "What's the matter?"

"I need to get rid of your coat."

And his smile was as the remembered sun had been before the coming of the storm, which was then still roaring gutturally and shrilly outside. He said to the neophyte, "Let me help you. Just relax. I can do this for you. Ahhh, I love your body on mine. Ummm. Give me just a little kiss."

Then after a while, he panted in gasps, "Who the hell taught you to kiss like that? Is he still around?"

"No."

"What else did he do to you?"

"Nothing. Obviously. I wouldn't be here—in bed with you—if I wasn't this curious."

She sounded just a tad huffy. So he said with silken tones, "I'd think of some way. I'm gonna git you."

"Maybe."

She was getting cold feet. Well, that was also true, but she was backing out. So, of course, he kissed her with tenderness. His hands moved only where they ought to be and he didn't allow them to get too fresh with her. He was courting. He was careful.

She was naked and so was he. His body was very sensitive to hers. He could feel her. He had her lying halfway on him again as he gave her a series of very interesting kisses. All were gentle and sweet. His hands were on her head and in her hair.

She knew he was making her hair a mess but she liked his hands on her head. Pretty soon, she wanted them on her back. She moved her head a little and that moved her shoulders so that her breasts wobbled on his chest.

She had him so triggered that he was about to blow steam—or something equally eruptive.

His voice was hoarse as he asked, "You okay?"

"Are you catching cold?"

"No. I'm just triggered so that I'm really very tense."

"From...what?"

"Lust."

She chuffed and then laughed over his distress. She was really amused.

That was better than hostility.

He kissed her sweetly and made relishing sounds. He moved his hands in a friendlier way. He got fresh.

She questioned such conduct. "Are you supposed to do that, this soon?"

"I've delayed it. I was so fascinated by your kisses that I forgot to pet you just right. How about that? Is that okay?"

"I'm not sure," she said thoughtfully in a very sly and enunciated manner. "Do it again."

So he did. He was very careful and wicked and exceptionally skilled.

She asked with narrow eyes, "Who taught you to do that?"

"That's how I make the dogs' eyes close in pleasure. I was just seeing if you're as smart as—"

"As smart as...what?" she asked a little stridently.

"—as you seem."

She wasn't entirely sure that had been what he meant, but then he kissed her again and he curled her toes and made her body really quite rash and somewhat crude.

He suggested quite logically, "Why don't you lie here where I am and let me get you even warmer?"

"Okay."

They shifted, and she was in the hot nest he'd vacated to her. She murmured sounds of pleasure. She did that just to be warm? What would she do when he made love to her?

He'd find out.

He went down under the covers and slid along her body. He said, "Don't pay any attention. I'm just being sure you're warm enough."

"Oh." She said that once. Then she said it in gasping breaths. Then she just gasped.

She was easy.

He was smiling, concealed under the covers that way. He did all sorts of things to her vulnerable body. And he came up her body to her chest and found her nipples all puffed and ready. He tasted them. He rubbed his smoothly shaven face on her chest. And he was loving her.

With his hands on the mattress and holding his weight, he came up her to her mouth. He kissed her as a woman ought to be kissed in those circumstances.

She became suspicious as to how innocent he might be. He was very skilled. Of course, he was just doing what seemed natural.

He was forward.

He whispered sweet words. One of his older friends had once told Kyle, "Never tell a woman to open her legs. She'll get defensive. Tell her to part her knees a little. To them knees aren't as vulnerable."

So Kyle said softly, "Part your knees."

She did.

And the next thing she knew, he was settled quite exactly and ready. She breathed and her breasts pushed against his chest. Her face was very serious and her eyes were simply enormous.

He kissed her sweetly as if that was all he wanted, right then. With the kisses, she relaxed a little and her fires became hot. She moaned a little wisp of sound.

It riveted Kyle.

He pressed his sex against her. And he asked in a husky whisper, "Want me?"

With his words, he remembered asking a woman that and she'd snorted before she replied, "What the hell do you think I'm in this position for?"

But Lauren said, "Yes."

He lifted his face to look at her and she returned the look very seriously. Her breaths had quickened.

So he told her, "Now you can put it in."

"You can't?"

"If I tried, I just might hurt you a little. You can slip it in."

"That seems rather pushy."

"I've never had a pushy woman. In the few that have accosted me, I was the victim. Be gentle."

And she accepted all that. She reached down and slid his slippery eager sex into her. It was blocked. But he worked it in carefully. And then he lay quietly, going crazy, but getting her used to him... enough.

Her breaths were emotional. She was one of those who was very aware of what was happening. It was different, and she was struck by the fact of what she was involved in right then and there.

She said, "I probably should have waited for a husband to do this."

And naturally, Kyle replied, "No, you needed this experience with me. After this, you'll understand it can be nice."

"Oh." Lauren blinked a time or two and then she wondered. "This is... nice?"

"You'll like it."

She turned her head so he raised his to see what she was doing. She was looking off to the side thoughtfully. She wasn't panting with passion. She wasn't being swamped by thrills. She was thoughtful.

He asked carefully, "What are you thinking?"

And she said, "I probably should have waited until after I was married."

In that position, Kyle was quick and earnest. He promised Lauren, "He'll never guess you've tried it. It's like with men. Nobody knows for sure."

So, in that position, she asked with interest, "How many women have you had?"

And he instantly replied, "None that I remember."

"I thought you said—"

"I was trying to be smooth and knowing." He then added, "Unless some woman used me when I was out cold some time or the other."

"When were you out cold?"

"Could we delay this discussion until another time? Say, tomorrow?"

"Why?"

"I could probably go on discussing these fascinating distractions, but Homer is hungry. He's in the right place for the first time I can remember, and he's getting anxious."

"Oh."

"Pretend you're having a good time and let me make love to you."

"What all do I have to do?"

He paused and levered himself up on his elbows. He was triggered so that his sweaty hair trembled. He was serious. "That doesn't sound like passion. That sounds like tolerance."

"Uhhh—"

He urged, "Say that I'm the most fascinating man you've ever encountered."

Like a parrot, she said, "You're fascinating."

With tolerant impatience, he lectured, "Say the whole thing—that you've ever encountered."

"That I've ever encountered."

He sighed. "You're a slow study. I can't believe that a hot woman like you could be this dormant. Move your hips until you know where Homer is."

"Umph."

"Not *that* wild. You'll eject us!"

She giggled.

She was so amused that he caught it, and they both laughed. But then he kissed her. He settled in and really kissed her. He moved his hands and he moved Homer. And her attention became riveted to what they were doing.

His mouth was hot and he used it. He murmured his pleasure with her, to her. He moved his hands and he was admiring of her. He told her he'd never in all his life seen such a perfect woman.

He made love to her ears and to her eyes and to her mouth. His hands rubbed the sides of her breasts. And Homer was harder and bigger and pushier.

Lauren became riveted. She began to cooperate. Her body became a part of his. Her pleasure was stirred by Homer. Her breasts were titillated by Kyle's hairy chest. She moaned in pleasure.

And he took her all the way to paradise. And she had to struggle to catch up, but with his breaths furnace-hot, he waited for her. He touched and petted and held her. His kisses were dynamite. She was unstable. She gasped and moved and pulled at him.

And his laugh in his throat was the sexiest thing she'd ever heard in all her twenty-seven years. She hadn't known a man could laugh in such a way.

Finally, he asked, "Are you ready?"

She almost asked, *For what?* but he made it clear. She gasped, "Yes!" and they rode the glory trail together to exquisite release. They went on to wild surrender and to remarkable thrills that washed over their bodies, which they shared.

They slowed their movements, and finally they lay sprawled. They were so hot. But Kyle pulled the covers up over Lauren so that she would not cool too quickly and chill. He was sweating and his body was very slippery.

She twitched and rubbed against him, and he said, "Forget it."

Her laugh was wicked.

Sweaty and still hot, they lay and made throat sounds. They smiled and touched. He yawned. She was sleepy-eyed and smiling. She asked, "When can we do it again?"

He pretended to faint.

She said, "I would never have believed you could be a ham bone. You should have gone on stage."

"Homer is shy. I couldn't take him on stage. People wouldn't see me. He gets excited over anything."

"I hadn't noticed."

"You weren't looking."

She lifted the covers and put her head under them so that she could reach out and touch Homer. Kyle flinched.

She put her head out from the covers and asked, "What's the matter?"

"You just put Homer through a wringer and now you want to wobble him? He isn't ready."

"How long do I have to wait?"

Again, Kyle pretended to swoon. He did a brilliant job of it. For two seconds she got in a very alarmed gasp, but then she saw him peek at her.

After Kyle went to the bathroom, he came back to the bed. He lifted the covers without permission, and he was back with her. She laughed in her throat the way women do when they are pleased with a man.

They talked and sighed and smiled, and they finally slept. Outside, the storm shrieked and wailed and blew around the house, shaking it as the ice in the storm hit the surface of the barricade.

They were lucky to be in a house.

Eight

——

It wasn't too late in the day when Kyle and Lauren wakened in what was a cold room, but they were in a nice warm bed. The thick clouds of the mean storm made it seem later than it was.

The new lovers sighed and smiled at each other. Then Kyle looked at his watch. Why do men always look at their watches at such a time? It took a while because the light was poor.

They were so cozy under those heavy quilts. Lauren still had on his flannel shirt. It wasn't buttoned. Her feet were encased in his thick woolen socks. She moved and sighed in contentment.

She triggered Homer, but Kyle silently told his sex to back off. That led to a mental debate that amused Kyle. Homer asked how could he "back off" when he was as attached to Kyle as he—

Lauren said in a murmuring way, "I shouldn't have waited so long."

Kyle's bliss was jolted. He immediately told her with grave seriousness, "We waited for this time. It wouldn't have been as magical if we'd been sorting out partners and experimenting before now."

"You did."

How rude of her.

And he told her seriously, "Once I was a victim. I had no choice."

"Balderdash. You are too big and strong to be the victim of a woman's voracious lust. Don't try to tell me you were a victim."

He said earnestly, "Some women won't take no for an answer. They're pushy and mean."

She curled over to him and rubbed the magical hair on his chest and stomach. She told him intimately, "You would tempt any woman."

His voice was honest as he said earnestly, "I don't want just any woman."

"Then how come a woman could lure Homer and not you, as you claim?"

"A man hesitates to physically reject a woman. He could hurt an aggressive woman. She takes him by surprise. The woman who used Homer was a shock to me. I didn't even like her."

Caught by Kyle's earnestness, Lauren told him, "I never before thought of a man as being just . . . used."

"We're vulnerable." He was serious as he said the words, "You're a nice woman. Like the mean or wicked men in this world, there are mean and wicked women. They use men. It is true. There are women voyeurs who are just like such men. I've run into them. I had to learn how to protect myself."

Lauren replied, "I have trouble thinking about a women . . . using . . . you against your will."

"With an aggressive man, you can rough him up, but any man hates hurting a woman while he's defending himself. He can be charged with assault."

"What about Homer?" Lauren asked with real curiosity. "Was he shocked? Indignant? Did he go limp and faint?"

"Homer lives his own life. He can be lured against my rejection."

"Ahh!" she exclaimed, "Then I just need to work on Homer?"

"No. If you're serious about Homer, you have to work through me. We're an entity."

After a silence as she lay beside Kyle and petted his chest hair, she asked, "What did your daddy tell you about handling such an episode as you had?"

"He'd never run into anything like that. He was dog mad. We waited to see the testing. It was a tough time." Then Kyle told Lauren very seriously, "I'm clean."

She asked with curiosity, "How did you know that I was?"

He replied softly, "Everybody calls you the Virgin Queen. They've done that since you were Queen of the Fiesta when you were eighteen." Then he added softly with a throat clack of emotion, "I have proof you were a virgin."

"I suppose that would be a clue."

Kyle inquired with soft care, "Why did you wait for me?"

"You've just said it." She shrugged. "I was ready. I found you."

"Actually, I was the one who found you out there on that plain. You were really stupid to ignore the coming storm and try to get that damned pod. The only reason I don't scold you—"

"You are now."

"—is because I'm glad you did all that stupid stuff, and that I found you . . . in time. It would have killed my very soul if I'd stumbled onto you out there and you'd been dead. And frozen. Gone."

She slid in the comment, "It would have upset me a little, too."

"You were just this side of freezing. I saved your neck. Don't you forget that. You owe me."

She lifted her eyebrows in a very snubby manner and said, "I just paid you off with my precious body."

He hugged her closer and made male sounds of relish. "Let's do it again."

She sighed with dramatic endurance and inquired, "Just how many times will I have to 'do it' in order to pay off this burden of debt?"

"I'll keep track," he promised. Then he added, "And I'll let you know when you're debt free."

"That sounds rather vague and not at all original. Even banks tell you how long it'll be and how much. How long and how much will this rescue cost me?"

"I'll have to see how much you eat." He had to again look at his watch because he wasn't looking at time but at how long the roast had cooked. He told her kindly, "The potatoes and roast should be about done. Are you any good at making us a salad?"

In some obviously restrained brag, she replied, "Goldilocks does, on occasion, allow us to cut up the makings for a salad."

"Glory be."

She looked superior in a disgustingly elegant manner.

That made him laugh. Then he was generous: "You get to make the salad."

"I'm so grateful." She batted her eyelashes. "What sort of dressings do you have?"

"I got all the fixings."

Then he had to lie there and watch as she tried to dress without getting out of bed. She was fascinating! She wiggled and slithered and drove him absolutely wild.

So...when they finally got downstairs, the sweet potatoes had no resistance at all, to anything, and the meat was very well-done. But the salad was fresh and crisp. And she made biscuits. He was astonished. And he was cautious. The biscuits were absolutely delicious.

He asked, "Does...Goldilocks know about you making biscuits?"

"She broke her arm once. She sat and directed us all. I made the biscuits."

"What did your momma do?"

"She sat by Goldilocks and held her good hand. Mother is very compassionate with Goldilocks. She lives in terror that Goldilocks will up and leave us. We all have to be very kind to her and endure her criticisms and scoldings like ladies. That means we can't answer back."

"I didn't know ladies had rules."

She curled her fingers, just so, put the back of her hand to her forehead and shared. "It's a burden. I can hardly wait to marry and get out of the household."

"You're old enough to leave if you want to."

She went back to eating but said dismissively, "I'd be lonely. Being raised with all those people around was a thwarting to the urge for independence."

"You could come stay with me for a while. We could see how we rub together."

"That again."

"I'll behave for a while," he vowed rashly. "Think about moving out here."

With complete rebuttal, she replied a nothing, "Sure."

"What's that mean?"

She flopped her arms out in acceptance that it would be true and said, "My daddy would be out here with his shotgun. He's a hard-nosed man."

And Kyle said in a dead voice, "I'm terrified."

It was only then that Lauren realized Kyle could well be a match for her daddy. How strange. It was a fact that Kyle never would bow and scrape. He might not even listen to what her daddy had to say. How amazing. Out there in the sticks, she had met a man who not only wasn't interested in her daddy's money, but he didn't care what her daddy thought of him!

Could she be with a man who was indifferent to her father? And her humor jiggled around inside her. All that time she'd spent discarding men because they were awed by her daddy. Now, here was a man who didn't care two hoots? Shouldn't that offend her?

Was Kyle really indifferent to approval or was he just pretending to be interested only in her?

Yeah.

With the old Davie family businesses in TEXAS, it was vital to have the approval of the head of the woman's family. The petitioner needed the moral support in his ventures, and he needed the financial backup.

"You a loner?" She asked that with her head tilted back and her eyes slitted.

"I got one daddy. I don't need no more."

And she lied. She said, "My daddy backs me."

"He's why you were Queen of the Fiesta. He wanted it. You didn't."

She almost hid her surprise. "How'd you know that?"

With compassion, he told her earnestly, "I've never before seen such a straight standing, smiling young woman who was so miserable."

"How'd . . . you know . . . that?"

He said softly, "Your eyes."

Staunchly, she declared, "I did not shed one tear!"

How telling for her to admit that. He told her, "It took all your skill and discipline to keep those tears in your eyes."

She considered the time, almost ten years ago, and she remembered. "You might be right."

He took hold of her hand on the table. "I watched you. You were something to see. I could see you as a settler in this virgin, unclaimed land." Then he acknowledged honestly, "There were already nine hundred Indian tribes here in TEXAS when the Spanish arrived. The Indians tried their darnedest to keep us Europeans out. If you'd been here then, you'd have helped your man. You'd have been a backup for any man."

She shook her head. "I'm a total coward. How could you contrive all that balderdash?"

He replied easily, "I made a study of you then when you were queen."

"How?"

"I was a tad bored," he admitted with a shrug. "You were in the spotlight. I studied you because you're really something to look at. Then I studied you when I realized you didn't want to be there."

She scoffed. "You dreamed it all."

"At the club, I saw you save that dog from the guys who thought it was funny to sic it on a sick cat."

She hesitated before she commented, "I'd forgotten that." Then she asked, "You were at the club then? I don't remember seeing you there."

"I was on the screened porch just a way over. I told you later that I was proud of you. You blushed and discarded doing anything."

She looked up at his face. "I saw you then?"

"I'm a little older. You were of the age, then, as the nubile female who didn't notice older men. I was a guest. You were so positive in defense of the dog. I was impressed that the shrinking violet I had known could stand up for a dog. What else do you protect?"

"Carefully, just me. Back then, I wasn't at all brave. I don't like dogs particularly. I just thought the dog might get whatever disease the cat had."

"The grounds man solved them both."

Quickly, she protested, "I don't believe I want to hear how he did that."

"He called the shelter."

"Thank you."

"He really did. He's as tenderhearted as you. I once saw him cry over a dog hit by a car."

"Anybody does that. Dogs have wiggled their way into the human structure, and we accept them as needed creatures. They are a polluting nuisance. Their time is past."

He chuckled and tried not to. Then he laughed.

"Hush."

The dog chose that time to come into the kitchen. The hound came over wagging his tail as if they would celebrate seeing him.

Lauren asked, "How'd he get out of the storage room?" Then she gasped. "Someone is here!"

"I would doubt that. There's not been any call. And this dog opens doors."

"How?"

"With his mouth. And teeth. Every now and then I'm not wearing gloves and I find a doorknob all lathered with dog saliva."

"Ugh."

Kyle sat back and sighed in defeat. "Now, you'll be suspicious of all doorknobs and—"

In a companionable, friendly manner, the dog jumped up on the chair across the table.

Lauren screeched, "No!"

The dog was startled to be rejected. He just stood there unmoving. Like there was something *else* that was disturbing the woman? He looked around to see what it might be.

Kyle chided the dog, "You know better!"

And the dog got off the chair with an *Oh, yeah! I'd forgotten!* sort of laughing look.

Dogs are crafty and sly. And they push limits every time!

Come to think of it, so do men. They were very similar to dogs. They were susceptible to human females. They got in earnest or hilarious scraps. Yep. They even howl at the moon on occasion.

What was she doing in Kyle's house with him all this time? Well, outside that, she shouldn't be sharing his companionship this way. But with the storm, she could hardly say, 'Thanks for the experience. You did well" and leave... with that storm and her car somewhere else and filled with snow?

She looked at the covered windows but noted the small movement of the drapes as the storm's fierce winds found tiny cracks. It was cold.

She shivered and automatically wanted to have him against her as she sought his warmth. How shocking for her to do such? How could a man be so like a furnace? Ummmm. And her knees rubbed together discreetly. And she was sitting at the table.

Kyle told the dog, "Go back to the storage room— and close the door!"

The dog smiled as he wagged his tail. Then he went out of the room and on beyond. They heard nothing after that.

She inquired, "When did you know he could open and close doors?"

"Almost right away. I gave him a lecture on being sure the doors were closed. For a while he went around closing doors. Then I had to tell him to close them only if he had opened them. That took a while."

"Is he neutered?"

He was *aghast!* "Now how in this world could I do that to another dog?"

Did Kyle mean that he had neutered other dogs, or was he putting himself into the dog category? Did he realize he was one of them?

In those odd three days, the oddest thing was that they made ice cream. Yes. They could make ice cream because he hadn't had to turn off the gas. There was no need to half freeze her after she'd willingly slept with him. He even put the electricity back on.

Men are especially crafty around and about women. Women have to pay close attention to male conduct. Lauren wasn't very good in her judgment. She was grateful he'd found her on the plain, warmed her and brought her to his place.

She was even more grateful that he had been willing for her to experience him. Twice. Each time, she was amazed it could be so...nice. She was glad she hadn't tried it with any one else. Kyle was perfect.

Across the table from her, eating ice cream in spite of the storm, Kyle asked, "How did you hold out for so long? I'm glad you did, but how did you manage to...not?"

"I was called the Ice Princess?" That was the TEXAS do-you-understand questioning statement. "No guy expected me to. They'd go with me in order to catch my daddy's eye. They didn't court me for me, they just wanted to be my daddy's son-in-law."

"So if I'm going to catch your attention, I have to ignore your daddy?"

"That would help my confidence in myself. But he would be fascinated by you."

"You're a jewel." He rose from his place at the table and gathered up all his dishes and utensils.

So she automatically helped with the cleanup.

Kyle said, "I've got to go out and milk those cows. Want to come along?"

"No boots."

"I think my mama's are here. You all's feet are near the same size. Let me see."

He went from the kitchen, leaving the door to the hall open. It didn't occur to Lauren right away but eventually she realized the air from the hall was heated.

When he returned, she told him in delight, "The electricity is back on!"

He asked, "How did you know?"

"The hall's air was warmer, so I turned on the light, and it worked!"

He looked at the light with some irritation. She'd probably want her own bed in another room now. He assured her, "It's still cold. This has to be another Storm of the Century."

Considering, she speculated, "*The Storm of the Century!* Do you suppose every storm will be called the Storm of the Century until we get past the change in centuries?"

He pushed up his lower lip as he contemplated her premise. Then he said solidly, "We could do that more than likely."

He found the boots for her. They didn't fit too badly. And he saw to it that she was covered from the blowing winds and snow. The gloves on her hands were simply too large. She said they were warm. He frowned and wasn't sure she ought to be outside. He considered her so female and fragile.

She was someone he should protect. When had he ever wanted to be so protective? When had he felt the need to be a shield to a woman?

She was snippy. She told him, *"I am woman. I can roar."*

He asked, "Why do you want to roar? No close neighbors. And it's not that I'd mind, you understand, but I'm just curious."

"That's from a long-ago song about women standing on their own two feet and roaring."

"That right." Not a question, it was an acknowl-
edging statement.

She grinned and her eyes danced.

He asked carefully, "You gonna roar?"

"I just might. I've had my way, so far." She was just
so sassy.

He said, "Warn me so's I'm not too surprised, just
before you . . . roar."

"Okay."

He let her go with him to the barn. She was animated and cheeky with the freedom. She acted as if
she was the one who was in charge.

She went to the door and opened it. The winds
snatched it from her hand and it banged against the
wall. She staggered back and bumped against Kyle's
solid chest.

He said, "It's a fresh wind."

In shock, she retorted, "It's a storm!"

He nodded very agreeably and added, "I'd noticed."

It was roaring as if it was furious with all the land
and it was rattling its war clubs and threatening. It was
so huge and the winds were so strong in their gusting
that it was intimidating for her. He didn't seem to
mind the storm at all.

Kyle went to the wind side of her and took her arm.
His body would break the force of the gusting winds.
She followed him outside onto the screened porch. She
was glad for the boots he'd found that almost fit. The
snow had come through the screens and was swirled on
the floor of the porch.

It is shocking to a TEXAS woman to see such invading snow. Dust, a woman could understand, but
snow? She looked beyond. The dark clouds were very

low and visibility was limited. There was snow blown across in the distance between the house and the barn. The drifts were a surprise.

She asked, "Will the drifts be okay?"

And he replied easily, "They will for anybody worth their salt."

That salt comment went clear back to the times of the Romans when the men in wars were paid in salt. It was that precious. Lauren supposed it was easier to send some men out to the salt mines than it was to share the captured gold.

Kyle went first, breaking the trail for her. That was only right. But the wind was wicked and invigorating! She kept her head ducked because the blowing snow was harsh. They got to the barn, and Kyle got the door open. They stumbled inside.

The two cows and the horses looked at the invaders with mild curiosity. Several dogs came with wagging tails.

"Who piled the hay?" she asked. For it was baled and stacked against the northwest wall.

"That's a barrier for the wind in the wintertime. We have a long way to the northwest that is open and there's nothing to stop the winds. We've a couple of groves that we're getting started to slow it all down before it hits us thisaway."

The hay was loose in the loft. And Lauren gasped because there were chickens up there!

She asked, "Chickens?"

Kyle was courteously greeting the barn animals, the gathered horses and the dogs. He replied to her question, with another question, "Where do you think I'd get fresh eggs?"

"The grocery?"

"It's a way to there. This is handier."

He took off his coat and hung it from a peg on one of the stalls. He had a gun.

That was sobering. Why a gun? So of course, she asked. And he said, "You just never know who'll turn up. Best to be ready for it."

"Have . . . you ever . . . shot anyone?"

He promised seriously, "No women."

That wasn't particularly soothing. "Why. . . .did you . . . shoot anyone?"

"I found a guy trying to take my milk cow—this here is the one, her name is Sally."

Pale faced and with quite large eyes, she asked, "Did you—kill—the rustler?"

"Almost." He loved her serious word for the thieving man. "He'd hid a gun and gave me this." Kyle lifted his Stetson and showed a white line on his scalp. Obviously the thief had tried to kill Kyle!

She was soberly silent. She moved around. She spoke kindly to the dogs but she didn't touch them. They realized she didn't want to so they allowed her room enough.

Lauren watched Kyle with the animals. They loved him. He petted the cows enough. They turned their heads to watch him. The horses came and pushed to be petted. And the dogs stood around laughing silently with opened mouths and wagging tails.

How strange it was to her that all those bodies responded to Kyle's petting, to his touches, to being held and hugged. She understood. She liked his attention and touches, too. Did that mean she was also an animal? That she shared all the feelings of those speechless devotees? Probably.

So he loved the animals. He would be that way with children.

She was going rather rapidly down the mental road of knowing this man. She'd been with him for something over twenty-four hours. And she was considering what kind of daddy he'd be? It must be her age. She was ready to settle down and become a broody hen?

And she was amused by herself.

Kyle forked up the animal debris and spread clean straw on the barn's dirt floor.

She watched, then she went into the loft and found the eggs.

Kyle bragged on her, and she laughed.

Although the chickens weren't at all interested, the animals followed the pair to the barn door. None of them offered to follow the humans across the wind torn, snowy yard to the house. The animals nuzzled Kyle and the dogs put their heads under his hands.

Kyle rubbed them all. He talked to them and told them to keep warm and to protect the chickens. The dogs found that especially funny. The chickens never came out of the loft with the dogs down there.

So Kyle carried the pails of milk back to the house. He walked to her left to brunt the strong winds. And they got back okay.

He put the pails down on the porch and saw that she got inside the house all right. Then he went through another door to pour the milk into the big container. It would be collected by the next day if the roads were clear enough. In that room there was no heat and the milk was kept cold.

Kyle went back to the kitchen and shed his coat, muffler and hat. He put those on pegs by the door. Then he washed his hands. Drying them on a towel, he watched Lauren. He liked having her there.

Then he tried to remember any other woman he'd had there whom he'd wanted to stay with him. Not just be around for a while, but to stay. He wanted this one to stay.

It was dark by then. The winds kept it up. The whistling and moaning was interesting when one was inside and listening and not outside and coping. He wondered how the hands were doing. He wondered if they'd lost any of the beeves.

He was going to get the satellite cellular hookup. That would save a lot of wondering, worrying and time.

Lauren asked, "What has distracted you?"

He grinned. She liked his attention. He'd been distracted... from her. He said, "I'm thinking about getting a satellite cellular hookup, so the men can call in. They're trailing the herd and keeping the beeves from tumbling down or over anything. Rough work in this weather. It's good for them. It tests them."

"And you love it?"

He replied logically, "It's all I know."

"You went to school."

"I studied doing this." He lifted his hands out palm up to indicate what was around them.

"So you like this part of the world?"

She didn't? "Yeah." He said it soberly. So he asked, "You gonna marry me?" When she didn't respond instantly, he added, "You'd save me from other women."

She blinked. Then she smiled slightly and replied the ringer, "You'll have to ask my daddy."

"What if he says 'No.'"

"You'll have asked. I'll decide."

He smiled. He had a great smile. He said, "So you think it's all up to you?"

Studying him, her eyes smiling, she explained, "I have to know you better."

He was rather elaborately shocked. "How much better can you know me? I've shown you what all I can do. I can roll you around on the bed, and I can cook pretty good. I can ride a horse, drive a car and wrestle down any recalcitrant creature there is around here, and I can milk cows."

"We'll see what else you can do."

"Uh-oh, you're planning on putting me through the wringer?"

She soothed with some sassiness, "I'll try to keep you whole."

Nine

———

Kyle built a perfect fire. It was in the fireplace, naturally, and it was just right. Lauren put pillows from the sofas on the floor, but he put them back on the closest sofa and sat her there.

He explained logically, "We have to be comfortable. We're gonna watch the flames and decide what they mean and what they look like."

With interest, she said of her own family, "We never did that."

So he told her, "It's just a whole lot like being out on a hill and figuring out what the clouds look like." Then in an aside he admitted, "Most of those I've seen are triple X-rated."

"How shocking!" Really a fake exclamation. She needed practice.

He exclaimed, "Look! That tall flame? She's naked and writhing in lust."

Lauren stared. *And she could see exactly what he meant!* But she asked, "Where?"

"Over on the left. The tallest flame!"

She made a disbelieving sound quite well and retorted, "That's a waterfall."

He scoffed, "Nnn— Yeah! It is! It's fiery water rolling down her naked body. Wow!"

"I'll look for the man who's making her behave that way." She found a flame-toad sitting blunt and sleepy-eyed. "A toad. Not as big as the creature in the Star Wars series, but adequate."

He couldn't find it.

She looked for a dog. A big, dominating one. She found a man's flickering form hovering over a burning log whose low flame was a supine woman.

Lauren thought how strange she'd never seen such porn in any of the other fires she'd sat and watched. She'd never really looked at them with salacious interest?

She was looking then at the fire the hot man, next to her, holding her, had concocted. She saw a baby squatted down and reaching. Its attention was riveted on something. And her lips parted in alarm that the flame-child would be harmed...by the fire...of which it was a part?

The crackling of the flames was soothing. Was it because, down through the ages, fire had been such a precious, needed part of human lives? Or was it because it was so comforting that there was the bonding with a controlled, deliberate fire?

Lauren asked, "Where do you get your wood for the fire?"

Kyle shrugged. "Debris—storms."

"Trees are getting scarce." She felt the need to inform him of that problem.

He knew. He said, "We have more mesquites than anybody needs."

"They do survive," she agreed. "Keep some."

"Okay."

She explained to him, "You can plant oaks and hackberry and pines."

He rubbed his cheek against the top of her head. "We grow trees. We now fence off portions of our land to protect the trees when they're young. It'll be twenty years before they're big enough that we open it back to the cattle. In that time, we'll fence off other sections. We are very aware of how precious trees have become."

When they could no longer hold their eyes open, Kyle said he had to check on the barn. He'd take the dog with him. He left the gun with Lauren. "Do you know how to use it?"

Lauren frowned as she looked at Kyle. "What all do you want me to shoot?"

So he took her out onto the back screened porch. There, he opened the far door. Then he came back beside her before he suggested, "Hit that nub on the bottom branch."

She hit the branch next to it. She hadn't considered the force of the wind on the bullet, at that distance.

He went to the barn after he admonished her to keep the door locked and gave her a signal that she would recognize as his. After a while, he knocked the three knocks they'd agreed on. Then he knocked once.

She let him inside.

"Well, I am certainly glad you allowed me back inside." Kyle was so earnest. "The barn would be a lonely place to spend the night."

She scoffed, "With all those animals?"

He slowly shook his head as he said very seriously, "None of them, not one of them . . . strips."

She tilted back her head. "Neither do I. Not after today's romps. Forget it."

As they went up the stairs to bed, he asked Lauren, "Which room?"

She became very serious. He was going to let her sleep alone in that big house? So she soberly looked around, waiting for him to suggest she just sleep with him.

He waited . . . silently.

Finally, she gestured minimally to the last room upstairs. He walked to the doorway and looked at it. Then he shook his head and said, "No sheets."

"You only have one pair of sheets?" She was unbelieving.

"How many do we need?"

She smiled a little. "Choose a room for me."

"We'll try this one."

With his comment on no sheets, she inquired, "Are there sheets?"

And he bobbed his head seriously. "I changed them when you were showering."

She nodded slowly. They would sleep together. How could her sated body be so pleased? He was warm. He'd keep her from freezing? The furnace was back working. It was cool but not cold in the house. She didn't need him to warm her.

She wouldn't mention that.

* * *

It was just a good thing they'd gone to bed fairly early. He was greedy. She laughed the first time. The second she murmured and nuzzled him. The third time she asked, "Been alone a lot lately?"

But that last time, at dawn, she never really wakened enough to help with her seduction. He didn't need any help. Her night was cozy and loving. And she was warm.

When she wakened in the silence the next morning, she couldn't sort out what was different. He was gone. That's what was different.

How could thirty some hours, glued to a man, make that normal? She was alone. No. The dog was on the bottom of the bed.

With stern censor, she asked the dog, "Are you supposed to be on the bed?"

He stretched and sighed in a tired way. Then he closed his eyes.

She watched him. He opened his eyes a little to see what she was doing.

She said, "Get off the bed."

The dog lay back and sighed mightily. Then he heaved up as if he weighed three hundred pounds and couldn't possibly move, but he was trying.

She didn't deter him. He stood like the statue of the last Indian's horse, head down, exhausted, but she said no more than, "Get off the bed."

He was a ham bone. He went carefully to the edge of the bed and looked into the abyss.

Again, she said, "Get off the bed."

He tried to find a careful way. He was brilliant.

She said, *"Git!"*

He stretched one foot down and tested the strength
of the floor, then he carefully put down the other front
foot and stayed that way, half on and half off, but she
said, *"Git!"* again.

The dog allowed his back feet to join the front ones
on the floor and he stayed bent up that way with all
fours on a very small portion of the floor, like it was
an ice floe on an ice-clogged, rushing river.

Lauren's eyes looked up to see Kyle in the doorway,
watching. She asked, "Is he a movie dog?"

"No. He does all that from his own imagination. He
is entertaining. That's why I brought him into the
house. I figured when you got bored with me and lost
interest, he'd distract you and entertain you all the
while when I was using your body."

"You've sure enough done that. How come you
could walk clear over there?"

"Homer let me get out of bed. You've worn him to
a nub. I ought to be able to control my own life now
for a couple of hours—while he recoups."

"Do all men name their—their—uh . . ."

"Sex?"

She blushed.

He bit his grin and replied, "The guys I know did.
Sex has a mind of its own. We males struggle against
it for civilized control."

"You're not sixteen."

"Yeah. I thought I was passing that stage just recently, but then I met you and Homer just—took
over." Kyle spread out his arms in a manner that re-
vealed all his tribulations.

She laughed.

He came over to the bed, pushing the oddly positioned dog away on the floor, and he took over the bed and its squealing-laughing occupant.

Eventually, he swatted her bottom in a very satisfied manner and told her, "Get up and greet the day! I'm gonna make tortillas for breakfast."

For... breakfast. She again tried to remember if she'd ever before eaten tortillas for breakfast. Well, in for a penny, in for a pound. She got up.

Kyle wanted to shower with her. She was wobbled. Shower? So she was washed selectively and her hair was a mess!

He dried her hair with a strange and reluctant blower one of his sisters had thrown away. He assured Lauren, "It works. It's just a little eccentric."

It didn't blow any fuses.

He put a soft, feather pillow on her chair. It was a good move. She sat and he made the tortillas from scratch. The were results were a little odd but actually delicious. She knew they were because she got one of the first ones to "test" it.

He'd watched her eat the tortilla. She had been rather elaborately studying and contemplative. She had tilted her head and squinted her eyes as she chewed. She'd finally nodded her head in acceptance.

And he laughed. He mussed her hair, and she protested. He said he'd curry it. She replied, no, thanks, anyway. He said she was selfish. How else was he to do something in order to understand horses' tails?

She threw the morning paper at him.

The morning paper? She looked around and listened. The sounds of the storm were gone.

She got up from the chair quite slowly and quietly went to the west kitchen window. All was peaceful. The western sky was coming on as blue. The storm was over. She turned and just looked at Kyle. It was over. The storm, being isolated with Kyle—that magical interlude was finished.

He instantly told her, "We have snowdrifts."

"Does the phone work?"

He didn't reply for several long seconds, then he said, "I'll check it."

"I need to call Goldilocks. How long before I can get out of here?"

His face went past serious and became sad. "Pretty soon. I'll have to check it."

"My car—"

"I called to have it towed." He had just admitted the phone had worked. He held his breath. "I called almost right away when you got here." There, she would believe that he hadn't tried the phone since.

"I wonder if anyone will ever be able to drive it again." She was woeful.

And he comforted her, "It'd just gotten a little wet. Nothing fell on it or battered it."

"Oh."

Then he changed the subject with some determination. "Would you like some more tortillas?"

She was hesitant. "Do you know that Goldilocks hasn't ever given us tortillas for breakfast?"

He was solemn. "Your family has been deprived. You're in for a treat."

The egg was fried solid so nothing could leak, and the bacon was crisp. Lauren eyed the chili sauce with some hesitation, but Kyle was cautious with the neophyte. He rolled the ingredients into the hot tortilla, and handed it to Lauren.

It was delicious.

She had, for Pete's sake, three of the combination. It was a good thing the storm was past. She was free to leave.

She glanced over at Kyle.

He was watching her with serious eyes.

The rising sun was determined to show through the tiny holes in the eastern, disintegrating clouds. How TEXAS of it.

She went to the back door and opened it. It was cool outside. Not the bitter storm cold, but just cool. The breeze was determinedly balmy. She saw it was having an effect on the snow. So soon. The snow would be melted by the end of that very day.

How sobering. How could she claim to be trapped there without any snow? Of course. She didn't have her car. She turned to Kyle. "Does your car work?"

He thought of the gem in the shed. "No. Something went wrong, and I've been trying to figure it out."

"I'll call Goldilocks."

"I don't think they've fixed all the lines yet. It's being called the Storm of the Century."

"Goldilocks said that."

"Want another tortilla? I made a batch."

"I would like to be able to stand up and to try to walk a little. What with one thing—" *him* "—and another—" *the food* "—I find walking rather odd."

"I'll carry you. Where do you want to go?"

She smiled on him. And a brief sunbeam came into the room. It had been there for a while; he just thought it was her smile that had brightened the room.

From the other side of the table, he asked her very nicely, "Will you marry me?"

"You'll have to ask Daddy first. I've already told you that."

Being a pushy, obstinate man, he pushed, "But are you willing?"

"I suppose that would enter in. I do like you. I love the way you use my body and—"

He sighed. "That's just sex."

"We probably need to see if we rub nicely in other ways."

His eyes were vivid. "How?"

She chided, "I was speaking of parties, lunches, golf, that sort of thing."

"I'm lousy at golf. I can't find any real reason to follow a ball around a mowed land with cups—hidden—here and there."

"People play golf so that they can bond."

"I suppose."

"If golf doesn't grab you, what does?"

"Rodeos."

"Those are absolutely dangerous. I forbid you participating in such madness!"

He loved it. "Well, okay."

She brightened. "Promise?"

He was careful to appear reluctant. "Okay."

She leaned to him and kissed his ch— Mouth! He *was* quick! She said, "You darling! I know it would be tough for you, but I am so glad you understand. If you were hurt, I'd be upset."

So would she be . . . upset. He hadn't been in a rodeo since he was twenty-five and finally realized binding the horses and bulls thataway was mean and what he was doing was a tad stupid!

But she didn't know that and she smiled so tenderly at him that he had to get up and scoop her from the chair and sit down with her on his lap. That dumb Homer was vividly alert, but Kyle was in control.

Kyle was no dog. He was a good man.

He said, "I haven't had much experience with daddies. How do I approach yours?"

"We need to know each other better."

"That again." He sighed dramatically.

That was when she became serious about him. There had been his care and tolerance of the dog. His care and tolerance of her. His intent attention. His willingness.

She would have to know how he was when he wasn't so hungry for her. She would have to see how he was with her family. With her friends. And she said, "We need to know each other better. Three days in a snowstorm are too unique. We need some normal time."

Dramatically, he put his hands into his hair and leaned over as if in pain as he said, "I knew it! You *are* a stickler!"

She loved it.

"What would your mama think if you took me home to her and said, 'This is my old lady.' "

And Kyle replied kindly, "She'd say, 'Thank the Lord he's legit.' "

She tilted her head, squeezing her lips into a bud to keep from laughing. She managed to comment quite steadily, "She knows you."

"She's been after me to get married ever since I was about sixteen."

"Sixteen!"

"She wanted me out of the house, legit. She couldn't run me out—to get rid of me—and not have everybody know she was fed up with me. Any female knowing all that just might hesitate getting involved with me."

"What...all...were you doing?"

He was open and honest. "Being reasonable. She was a dictator. She wanted us to do things right then and we had other things to do. She didn't understand anything at all."

"Like—?"

"The pin ball machines, girls, the computer dungeons and dragons—"

"Yes." She was compassionate.

"And what she wanted was shoveling out the barn and cleaning out the well and things like that there."

"Mothers are insensitive."

"My dad sent me to sea for a year when I got to be twenty and decided to run my life my way."

"Did it work?"

"Yeah. How would we be with children?" And he waited for her reply.

She honestly considered for a while. And he allowed her the time. Then she slowly replied, "Probably just like our parents."

He nodded soberly. "Just lately, I've noticed some of my dad's thinking mixed in with my own. His logic pushes right into my head and takes control! It is the weirdest thing I've ever experienced."

She sighed. "I'm more like Goldilocks."

"I've got to meet her and see what I could be getting into."

"Ah-HAH!" she ah-hahed. "I knew it! You're sexually tired and now you're backing out!"

He shrugged. "My sex-cleared brain has mentioned there's more to rubbing together than just sex."

She laughed.

If ever there'd been any question in his mind, that one response of hers would have washed such away.

Then he mentioned in a warning, "Your daddy could pull me through a knothole."

"Pay him no never mind. Seeing him is just a courtesy. Just don't argue with him. He can outargue *anybody*. Tell him what you want him to know, and don't tell him everything he wants to know. Don't bare your soul. Just let him know we're interested in each other.

"And for Pete's sake, don't tell him we've known each other... intimately. It's none of his business. If Daddy knew, he'd go through all his closets and the attic looking for the gun. It was really Mama's Alamo ancestors. She should have given it to the museum some long time ago. It's in mint condition. It works, if you have the correct loading materials.

"My daddy's people were out west and heard about the Siege of the Alamo. That great-granddad brought his two sons riding in. The war was over by the time they had heard and could get there but it was night when they did get to the Alamo. A nervous Mexican had given up his arms but his had a lance. As horse-riding men came through his area, the Mexican threw the lance at them and hit my great-granddaddy, who was eighteen at the time."

And she sighed as she added, "Isn't it baffling how wars never seem to solve anything?"

He was serious. "Maybe it's an implant-population control solution." And he inquired, "What else do you think about when you're alone and bored?"

She considered. "It depends on why I'm alone and bored."

"Does it happen often?"

She supplied, "Waiting for my sister who is always late. She can't figure out what to wear."

"One of my brothers has a wife who's like that."

And they talked about all sorts of things. They gave opinions and found they could be on opposite sides without being hostile. They found they mostly agreed. They grinned at each other.

They watched the taggle ends of the storm leave them.

They didn't mention the fact that the storm was leaving, they tried to distract each other from knowing. Recognizing that fact would mean the end of their time together. That magical three days of Paradise. She would have no reason to stay. And he had chores.

Then some of his crew came back. They were in the barnyard, noisy and tired. Kyle had to go out and talk to them.

At some distance back from the window, Lauren watched as Kyle met with the other men. They looked at the house. They leaned forward to hear what he said, but they kept looking at the house. Kyle was talking about her.

The men were curious. Kyle was gesturing to the barn and on beyond to the hill where their quarters were. He was telling them to go get some sleep.

Well, he was telling them to go someplace else, not to the house.

Lauren was thankful for that much. It was bad enough to be caught in a house alone three days with a man, and nobody else was anywhere around. They'd know she had to have been there since just before the storm had hit. There'd been no other way for her to get there through the snow.

She'd been in that house—with Kyle—for three days. Three whole, almost entire days.

The men would wonder about what all they had—done—together.

And how could she not blush and be cool like she'd not been fooling around with the man who had been with her? How could she handle it?

Probably not at all well. And she couldn't face them with calm coolness. She'd blush. She was grateful Kyle was smart enough to funnel the men off to their quarters.

Men gossip.

Men tell things to other men and her daddy would be hearing about all this in probably just something like fifteen more minutes! Just watch. The phone would start ringing there at Kyle's. And all sorts of people would be saying, "Uh, is Lauren Davie there?"

And her daddy would probably be at least the second call. He'd more than likely be the first—

And the phone rang!

It had begun.

Lauren's face was stark. She felt the blood all drain down into her feet. That would probably burst her shoes. And more than likely, with her blood all in her feet, she would probably faint.

How would Kyle react to her white, bloodless body, and scarlet feet, lying on his kitchen floor?

He'd probably take her out and bury her on the plain where he found her. That way, he wouldn't have to cope with explanations.

The phone finally quit.

Kyle walked different as he came back to the house. The only description she could find was that he appeared cocky. Well, he was certainly that.

She didn't open the door for him. It was enough that he'd told the men she was there. If she then had the door open for him, they'd think she was his slave... already.

Of course, she was not his slave. Not in any way. She was her own independent self.

Kyle came into the house, and she stood across the room and said nothing.

He told her, "We lost a cow somehow. Nobody can find her. All the other beeves had a nice walk and are coming back with the rest of the crew. They'll look for the cow along the way."

Seriously TEXAN, she stated, "In that storm, only one cow lost is not a bad deal."

"Every creature is precious." Kyle was steadily watching her.

"I need to go home."

"Your car can be delivered here. I'll call the garage."

Watching him earnestly, she said, "I appreciate the fact that you were smart enough to call them. Thank you." She did not want it delivered there. It would make it so blatant where she'd been for *three days*. She asked her host, "Is it at all possible for you to take me to my car?"

He was very serious. "I'd be honored. You left your keys in the car."

She admitted it in a convoluted manner, "I hadn't thought I'd not be right back."

He nodded seriously, "People tend to think that way. How soon are you coming back here?"

She lowered her lashes. He figured she was going to lie. He waited, watching her.

She told Kyle, "I have to check in at home. Could you come to dinner on Friday?"

His smile was slow but it was such a wonderful beaming look. "I would be honored."

"It'll be ghastly for you," she told him earnestly, shaking her head. "I'll have to mention where I've been these three days and how I've come to know you. They'll all be so curious about you."

He grinned. "Tell them about knowing me when I was in your court, back then, at the Fiesta. We're old acquaintances."

Her eyes opened and she looked at him as if he was a genius and not the sly dog he actually was. She said, "Good thinking. I'll do that."

He got his car from the shed and drove it around to the front door of the house. He had a hard time opening the front door because nobody ever used it. But the front door was on the other side of the house and he didn't want the yahoos out behind there to be straining their necks to get a glimpse of her.

As they drove along toward the garage, it was without much conversation. And she wondered if the magic was gone for them. Would reality ruin what they'd had?

What, exactly, had they had? They'd taken a lot of time to introduce her into the varieties of sex. It had been a crash course. Fast, quick, intense and multiple specific lessons.

She looked over at Kyle. It had been remarkable. He was so sweet. The whole three days, he'd been so darling. He could still walk.

Think of her being alone with him all that while. How had her guardian managed it? And her guardian made a really snotty sound in her ear.

So the cosmic happening hadn't been the maneuverings of her guardian after all. Who had been responsible? What brilliant spirits had contrived for Kyle to find and rescue her in those awful, potentially tragic circumstances? Without him, she could have eventually frozen to death.

And her guardian admitted to that part.

Lauren looked over at the skillfully driving Kyle. "Have I thanked you for saving my neck? God only knows what would have happened to me if you hadn't found— I forgot to get the pod! It's still on the table!"

He reacted with a perfect surprise. "Well, I could bring it into town the next time I come."

"On Friday?"

"If I bring you the pod, your parents could well inquire how I managed to get it."

"Uh-oh."

"We'll think of something." And he smiled at her. If she hadn't seen the wickedness in his eyes, he would have looked benign and helpful. He had deliberately not reminded her of the pod.

Ten

Kyle drove Lauren along the road that led from his house. He instructed her in exactly where she was, so that she could come back to him. If she would. Now that she'd had a wild sexual experience from a skilled man—and liked it—would she go berserk or would she feel attached to him?

Since Lauren would pick up her own car at the garage, at the crossroads, there was no reason for Kyle to follow her home. But before they got to the garage, he pulled onto a weedy, two rutted, side track and stopped. He sat back and quite seriously looked over at her and said, "You haven't thanked me properly for saving your neck."

And she sassed, "I've done nothing *else!* I've been on my back every single minute, just about."

"You ate, sitting at the table."

"On a pillow," she reminded him prissily.

"I was being courteous and kind."

She grinned at him. "You've been an attentive host. You will note the word?"

"Did you want to be ignored?"

She shook her head.

He said, "I'm going to miss you."

"Come see me."

He coaxed unfairly, "Why don't you just stay out here, with me?"

"My momma would have a conniption fit."

"What's gonna happen to you and me?"

She did ask, "You'll come to dinner on Friday of next week?"

"I'll be there. What time?"

"Papa always eats exactly at six. He's a pain in Momma's neck."

So Kyle looked off in the considering way of men, and he said musingly, "I can see eating at six."

"It's an uncouth hour."

His voice was smoky as he told her, "With you, no hour is uncouth."

"Your compliment was smooth and just right." She nodded and her face was smug.

He promised, "I'll try to remember what all my momma tried to grind into my head all those early years ago."

"I know of your momma and your sisters. I was too young for them at that time. Now, we might be friends."

"They'll love you." He smiled at her. "Or I'll break their necks."

"My family will take up with you like you've lived in our bosom all of our lives."

He said thoughtfully nodding, "I can handle bosoms."

"Watch it."

"I do. I do." But his wicked eyes laughed at her. He was so amused by his teasing.

Earnestly, Lauren told Kyle, "The only one you have to watch out for is my daddy. He's just so hardnosed and difficult and dictatorial. I don't see how momma has ever put up with him all these years."

And she felt that the intimacy they had shared allowed her a more open comment. "I wouldn't be married to a man like my daddy for all the money in this world."

Then she considered slowly, "I can be his daughter. He leaves us girls to Momma." After a thoughtful pause, Lauren mentioned, "Of course, she turns us over to Goldilocks."

Kyle put in, "I'm anticipating meeting Goldilocks."

Lauren sighed in satisfaction, "You're in for a treat."

Then they spent about an hour there in that weed-overgrown track, saying goodbye. Anyone standing around waiting for that to be accomplished would have thought they were parting forever.

When they were finally on their way to the garage again, around her lips the whisker burn was even worse. He stopped the car and got out a shoe shine container that carried cow balm for utters. It was what made his hands smooth. Well, smoother.

And the balm did help her face.

Everybody at the garage knew the convertible was that of a woman Kyle knew and probably one who had been stranded with him at his house during the Storm.

There was a gathering of idle men who were almost discreet in looking her over. They watched, cleared their throats and exchanged looks with one another.

They all saw her subtly abraded face. That perked them up. They shifted their feet and smiled and caught glances with their cohorts. And they all managed to individually greet Kyle, while Lauren really didn't notice any of them.

Women just learn early not to pay direct attention to strange, human males or unknown dogs. Especially rabid ones.

Her car had been rescued early enough that it was fine. Kyle had even had the gas tank filled. That had not only been his usual generous self, but it had indicated that he knew Lauren Davie well enough to have her car checked out and filled with gas. It was a subtle possessive indication of a man with a woman.

It fascinated the idle males. One had come through such snowdrifts he'd had to shovel an occasional path to get the pickup through, in order to be there when Kyle picked up one of the Davie girls' cars.

Obviously, not a whole lot was going on in the countryside at that time, in that area, and anyway they could talk about how the Storm had boxed them in. Each had at least one storm story. And they could nod in understanding over the brags of the others.

"I don't know how I ever got that damned bovine out of that there drift at that particular time!"

He had a reply: "You coulda jest left 'er there for the thaw. You had to know it'd melt right away."

And another couldn't resist. "Yeah, and you coulda milked ice cream!"

That got a patient laugh.

But with Kyle bringing one of the Davie girls for her car—after three days—there was silence. Smiles. Exchanged looks among themselves. And nobody spit their tobacco juice. Amazing.

She was wearing those silks.

Well, one spit discreetly when the juice began to run out of the side of his mouth. He was couth about it. He wiped his mouth with a bandana.

His wife probably would raise holy hell when she found that in the laundry.

Kyle understood the fascination of the watchers. But at that particular time, he wished them in Tripoli. He was reluctant to give Lauren up, even for a while.

He wondered soberly what their next meeting would be like away from his place and in other circumstances. He would look rough and uncouth at her house.

If she'd wanted a smooth lap dog, she could have married any of those barking as they had chased after her before then.

He was himself.

Kyle watched her with troubled possessiveness. Would he lose her? Would he only be remembered because he'd been her first? She liked it so much, she would probably loosen her chains of conduct and go try just about any willing man.

Another man could get her.

For some reason that made the skin on Kyle's back prickle and shiver. He needed to be around her in order to protect her.

She'd done pretty well by herself. She'd only three days ago gotten interested. And that had been with him.

She came to him and said, "You shouldn't have paid the tow."

Kyle replied very seriously, "You're my guest."

"Thank you."

He urged, "You're welcome to come back, now."

"Silly. You know I have to go home or Goldilocks will send out the Marines?" That was the do-you-understand questioning statement.

He assured her, "I was with the Marines in Desert Storm. If they came to my place, they would have a cup of coffee and go back saying they couldn't find you."

She nodded. She saw only him. She hadn't noticed all the yahoos who'd gathered to just look at her. They were shadows. Even Sam Books was there. He was an old goat who never left his place. But he was there to see the Davie girl.

It was ghastly for the new lovers to say a discreet goodbye. They didn't kiss. Her face was pink. The cow balm had helped but her face was still pink. She could be blushing.

Kyle took her to her car, and he put her in it silently. What could he add to all he'd already said? And he watched her leave.

She almost didn't make the first turn. She was still looking in the rearview mirror at him standing back there at the garage still watching after her.

She opened the windows because the breeze from driving would keep her eyes from tearing and distract her concentration on being with Kyle. She took off her sunglasses and let her eyes cope with the winds.

She wondered if she met Kyle under ordinary circumstances, would he still be as magical? Or had it been a half-frozen woman, lost, whose gratitude for

surcease and protection had taken over and over-
whelmed her?

Lauren's mother wasn't home. So Lauren went into
the kitchen and there was Goldilocks stirring something voodooed on the great gas range. She had her
black hair in multiple tiny braids and her stance was
intimidating.

Goldilocks frowned on Lauren and asked, in slow
up and down with every other word, "What have you
been doing?"

The vocal selection of "What you doing" was em-
phasized nicely.

"You know I was stranded in the storm."

"You okay?"

"Yes, of course." And naturally, she blushed. But
then her mouth just went on and told just about everything. Not the sex. Just the saving, harboring and
care. It spilled out of her like the fizz out of a jolted
bottle.

Goldilocks listened. Her big eyes turned on Lauren
from time to time and observed the talking Lauren.

And Lauren remembered all the times she'd come
home full to bursting of talk, her mother had been
gone, and Goldilocks had listened. How amazing to
realize that Goldilocks was the one who'd guided her
along her way.

Lauren didn't mention sleeping in the same bed with
Kyle.

As Goldilocks kept track of all the cooking and
baking she was doing, Lauren babbled on and on
about how Kyle had saved her life, finding her and
getting her warm. She told about Kyle's care and food
and concern, and how he'd saved her car.

Working at her pace, Goldilocks listened to Lauren and finally commented, "We gonna get to see this paragon?"

And with snippy teasing, Lauren retorted, "I haven't yet asked him!"

"You bringing him home for us to see if he's any good at all?"

"Next Friday for supper. All right?"

"We'll have fish. Catfish. Willard'll get us some. We'll snare him in with food. Men all like food and their stomachs make them think the girl is the cook."

Lauren protested, "I *could* have been as good as you—almost—if you'd ever let me try!"

Goldilocks lectured as she wobbled a long-handled spoon at Lauren. "You're the type that'll take over and run the place. I couldn't allow that in my kitchen. You'd'a been underfoot the whole, entire time!"

"I could have done it all."

"Your momma woulda sent you off to a convent instead of losing me. Keeping you out of the kitchen kept you from the convent."

"Glory be."

"Don't be snotty. I saved your skin."

So Lauren hugged Goldilocks who scolded, "Cut that out, this minute! What do you think I am? Shoo! Vamoose! Get yourself out of here."

And laughing, Lauren left.

So that evening, Kyle came into San Antonio and to the Davie house to see Lauren. Nobody of the family was there except for Goldilocks. She was in the den watching TV, so the two joined her. They held hands discreetly, and they didn't pay much attention to what was on the television.

They had no idea Goldilocks watched them the entire time.

After Kyle left discreetly, Goldilocks said to Lauren, "Looks to me like you got a good one. You locked him in yet?"

With some drollness, Lauren replied, "I haven't yet asked him."

And Goldilocks warned, "Don't fool around and lose him."

It was the next day that Lauren found her mother dressing to go out. She sat on the perfectly made double big bed that was her parents' resting place, and she asked, "What did you say to daddy when the cattle froze that time and he was yelling?"

"I didn't say anything. I just listened."

"He was so furious!"

"All men are, now and then."

"What did you say?"

"That it didn't matter all that much."

"You told him that?"

"I'd waited until he was just about finished with his yelling. He'd needed to do that. Then I told him that it wasn't fatal to us. We could handle it. That the frozen beeves would be butchered and given to needy people. He could take it off his taxes."

And the second oldest finally asked her mother, "And another time, when he was furious about Maribelle running off for that weekend with Talbert. What did you say that calmed him down?"

Her mother asked, "How old are you again?"

"I'm already twenty-seven."

"Then you're old enough. I reminded him of the weekend we ran off and Daddy came with his shotgun."

"Did you do *that?*"

Her naughty mother tilted her head. "I knew I had him. So I pretended it was all *his* idea. And when Maribelle came home and said she'd been at the Finkles, your daddy asked, "How are they?""

"Maribelle said, 'Fine.' And your daddy just let her walk on off up the stairs."

"Why didn't you scold her?"

"She'd found out Talbert wasn't for her. Sometimes that happens. A good woman has to get to know a man. If she doesn't, the marriage can be awful."

"So you promote women going off for weekends with a man to find out?"

"Never! I promote a woman to find out how a man really is. Sometimes a forced marriage doesn't work out at all well. A woman feels committed. She doesn't realize it's not wrong to admit the marriage won't work."

"How'd you know Daddy was the man for you?"

"He convinced me."

"How?"

"He really worked at seeing to it that I knew the kind of man he could be. How he treated animals, humans and women. Those are good tests. No woman wants an abusive man."

Lauren reminded her mother, "He yells."

"That's all he does. He has never hit *any*thing. He has yelled. He's yelled at you on occasion."

Lauren smiled and remembered. "When the boat turned over, and he didn't realize I wore an inflatable jacket."

"That was one time," Lauren's mother told her. "But do you remember when you went with Murdock? And he held you in his car? And wouldn't let you out?"

"The state cop came along and—Daddy sent him?"

"Yes."

"I'd never realized you all knew about that time. I've just blessed that curious cop!"

Rather stridently, her mother shared knowledge. "Parents have never had it easy."

Lauren shook her head. "I'm not sure I could handle all that with kids."

Her mother said softly, "They are so precious. It's worth the sweat."

And leaving that old time, Lauren put in what was important. "You haven't met Kyle."

"I look forward to seeing him." Then her mother asked, "Are you ... unsure about him?"

"He is the sweetest man."

"All men are sweet with a new woman."

"You offend him."

Her mother smiled. "So, you're his defender?"

"When you meet him, you will understand. I'm sorry you all were out when he was here last night."

"Friday will do."

"Your schedule filled until then?"

And her mother replied, "We'll let Kyle sweat a little. He will meet us."

"If you all are rude to him—"

"We've never been rude. You know that?"

Lauren was stubborn. "—I'll run away from home."

Her mother smiled. "Where would you go?"

"With him."

"Oops, this is more serious than I thought."

"He is perfect."

Gently, her mother cautioned, "NO one is perfect."

"Just you wait and see. He is."

When Kyle phoned, Lauren told him, "You have to court me."

"Golly, I haven't had to do that since high school. I'm not sure I can remember how."

"Send me flowers."

"What kind?"

"It doesn't matter. And come out here and call to me from the bushes."

"I think I've...outgrown that."

"Try." Then she asked, "Do you still have that pod?"

"Yeah. I'll bring it to you."

But he "forgot" and his surprise was quite honest looking as he apologized. But he hadn't forgotten, he'd just kept it as another excuse to see her again.

So on his own, Kyle went to her daddy's office to ask for Lauren's hand.

And her daddy sat back in his desk chair and squinted his eyes at the younger man. He asked, "How much do you need?"

Her lover was surprised. He asked a very puzzled, "What?"

And her daddy asked, "How much money does your spread need?"

With almost deadly courtesy, Kyle replied, "Nothing I can't handle."

"How much can you handle?" And Mr. Davie squinted his eyes just a little as he watched for squirmings.

"You trying to bribe me?"

When Mr. Davie just sat there, Kyle got up and left.

So that evening, as Kyle came to the Davie door, it opened before he even knocked. Lauren looked at Kyle with interest or maybe it was curiosity. She said, "My daddy has disowned me."

And Kyle grinned from ear to ear. "That gets him out of our hair."

She took Kyle out on the enclosed sun porch that was mostly glass walled. The place was large and there was a lot of furniture and potted palms. She found a niche for them behind some of the quite tall palms and sat down. She smiled up at him and patted the place next to her.

"Since you've been disowned, and I walked out on him at his office today, let's elope."

She sparkled.

Kyle went on, "I've got a license. You got to be checked out. It won't take long. Let's go."

"Everyone is going to be here for dinner on Friday. We can't sneak out now."

Kyle gestured openly, "You've been disowned, and I've been snubbed."

So Lauren was curious. "What all did you demand for daddy to get rid of me?"

He looked at her with indignation. "He wanted to know how much money I wanted to get from him along with you."

"How much did you demand?"

With some hostility, he said in dangerous softness, "Nothing."

Lauren was disgusted. She complained, "You probably could have gotten a cool million, they're so anxious for me to get married. You were rash to allow your indignation to get hold of you thataway."

"I don't need Davie money."

She sighed. "My granddaddy left each of us kids some stock. We get it when we marry. You'll have to just be kind about it . . . and accepting."

"The money is yours. You can do whatall you want with it, if it's gonna be forced on you. I won't touch it."

She observed him down her nose, then she declared, "I predict quarrels."

"Not with me, you don't."

She considered him. "I love you. I thought it was just the remarkable sex, but I have discovered there's more to you than just that."

Kyle was indignant and demanded, "*Just* that? Whaddaya mean—*just* that?"

And the humor bubbled inside her.

He frowned at her. "For a woman whose daddy has disowned her, you're pretty snippy."

She explained with airy shrugging, "He's done it before. He grew up without sisters and his mother died when he was young. Women baffle him." She smiled gently at Kyle.

"So you've decided to marry me without your daddy's blessing?"

"Goldilocks loves you."

He admonished, "I'm lovable."

"And I love you."

So he growled at her, "You're lucky I feel that same way about you."

"Really? I hadn't known you were emotionally involved."

And he demanded, "Be quiet and kiss me like you mean it. Kiss me with the passion you've been hiding from me. Kiss me, you wicked woman-trap."

His arms went around her and his breathing was harsh. His mouth rooted for hers and his body was intense.

She gave him a tiny little peck on his cheek and said, "Later."

He scowled and his eyes narrowed. "What do you mean . . . later?"

"After we're married."

"You're gonna be a holdout, until *then?*" His voice went way up.

"We'll be discreet," Lauren told him. Then she elaborated, "People are gossiping about my being in your house all that time." She slid a salacious look over at him and went on, "I said we made bread and kneaded it."

"I kneaded your body."

"I did notice you doing that," she admitted. "When you said you were going to take me to your 'place,' you were so ratty that I figured you were taking me to a line shack. And I knew you would keep me there as a love slave."

He nodded the entire time. "I very seriously considered it.

And she got leaky-eyed.

It was a terrible, emotionally exhausting time before they finally were married. And that was done with skill and pomp and circumstance. Goldilocks knew exactly what all to do, and she cooked a wedding breakfast that was superb. She had help. She'd chosen those aides. She ruled.

No one minded.

Their diverse relatives were not well acquainted with one another and within the year, three more weddings came from that encounter. It rather rattled both the Davie family *and* the Phillips'.

It's always risky to get strangers together. No one ever knows what will happen. But that's another story.

The two newlyweds honeymooned...in a line shack. She laughed and giggled and her eyes danced. If Kyle hadn't already loved her then, he would have after that reaction.

And he'd brought along the pod. They opened it carefully to see what waited there for their edification. It contained the figures 5 times 5 equals ?

That pod was what she'd risked her life to retrieve. The very stupidity of it all caused them both to be thoughtful. Their eyes met, and they considered one another in serious regard.

That coupling had been as chancy and as unplanned as the damned pod.

How strange that one such foolish adventure had led them into yet another. They touched hands and considered each other with sober evaluation.

Then they smiled.

They embraced with gentleness and relishing. They swam naked in the cattle watering hole. They rinsed off in the stored water.

They ate beans and bacon and the biscuits that Goldilocks had taught Lauren to make. They ate apples and oranges, and they did make love.

Ahhh, yes. The lovers did make love. And they laughed and teased and ran around naked.

It was the beginning of their long and interesting life. And their own children baffled and amazed and astonished them both in their close marriage that brimmed with love.

*   *   *   *   *

COMING NEXT MONTH FROM

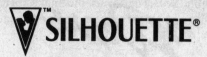

Sensation
A thrilling mix of passion, adventure and drama

NO MORE MISTER NICE GUY Linda Randall Wisdom
BROKEN SPURS BJ James
WILD BLOOD Naomi Horton
BRINGING BENJY HOME Kylie Brant

Intrigue
Danger, deception and desire

A BABY TO LOVE Susan Kearney
SEE ME IN YOUR DREAMS Patricia Rosemoor
A BABY'S CRY Amanda Stevens
CISCO'S WOMAN Aimée Thurlo

Special Edition
Satisfying romances packed with emotion

HONEYMOON HOTLINE Christine Rimmer
MAKING MEMORIES Ann Howard White
AFTER THAT NIGHT... Helen R. Myers
MARRIAGE MINDED Kayla Daniels
THE CASE OF THE ACCIDENTAL HEIRESS
Victoria Pade
MACKENZIE'S BABY Anne McAllister

COMING NEXT MONTH

STRYKER'S WIFE
Dixie Browning

Man of the Month

Kurt Stryker needed a wife. Since he had a really *hot* desire for Debranne Kiley it might as well be her. But if marriage was a shock for Kurt, then saying 'I love you' was going to be an even bigger one...

MONTANA FEVER
Jackie Merritt

Made in Montana

He was the best catch in the county—but Lola Fanon refused to be tempted by flirtatious Duke Sheridan. However, she was finding those brown eyes harder and harder to resist...how long before Duke got *his* way?

BACKFIRE
Metsy Hingle

Chase McAllister had manoeuvred Madeline Charbonnet from boardroom to bedroom but could he now go through with wreaking revenge on her father? Or had he messed up all his plans—by falling in love?

COMING NEXT MONTH

IN ROARED FLINT
Jan Hudson

Flint Durham had kidnapped Julie Stevens from her own wedding—and then proposed! Last time, he'd jilted her at the altar. So this time Julie wanted a level-headed stepfather for the twins—not one who set her heart aflutter and common sense askew...

MIDNIGHT BRIDE
Barbara McCauley

Sarah was half-naked and with no memory when Caleb Hunter found her. In his remote cabin, the two explored each other's bodies and hearts—but what waited in the real world to threaten their passionate paradise?

ABBIE AND THE COWBOY
Cathie Linz

Three Weddings and a Gift

When Dylan Janos whisked Abbie Turner away, she knew Dylan wasn't interested in settling down—just as she wasn't interested in a man like him. So why not just skip the wedding...and go straight onto the honeymoon!

LAURA VAN WORMER

◇

JURY DUTY

Dubbed the 'Poor Little Rich Boy' case,
this notorious trial will change forever the
lives of the twelve New York City
residents called to the jury.

*"A legal three-ring circus with brains and
wit, populated with colorful New Yorkers of
every stripe and class"*
—Kirkus Reviews

**AVAILABLE IN PAPERBACK
FROM FEBRUARY 1997**

New York Times bestselling author

LINDA HOWARD

ALL THAT GLITTERS

Married for love...or money?

Jessica had once been a wife in a marriage
rocked by scandal. But in Nikolas Constantino's
arms she found a peace she had never thought
possible.

"You just can't read one Linda Howard!"
—bestselling author Catherine Coulter

"Howard's writing is compelling"
—Publishers Weekly

MIRA®

AVAILABLE IN PAPERBACK
FROM MARCH 1997

SANDRA BROWN

New York Times bestselling author

HONOUR BOUND

Theirs was an impossible love

"One of fiction's brightest stars!"
—Dallas Morning News

Lucas Greywolf was Aislinn's forbidden fantasy—and every moment of their mad dash across Arizona drew her closer to this unyielding man.

AVAILABLE IN PAPERBACK
FROM MARCH 1997

FREE!

FOUR FREE
specially selected
Desire™ novels
<u>PLUS</u> a Mystery Gift
when you return this card...

Return this coupon and we'll send you 4 Silhouette Desire® novels and a mystery gift absolutely FREE! We'll even pay the postage and packing for you.

We're making you this offer to introduce you to the benefits of the Reader Service™ – FREE home delivery of brand-new Silhouette novels, at least a month before they are available in the shops, FREE gifts and a monthly Newsletter packed with information, competitions, author pages and lots more...

Accepting these FREE books and gift places you under no obligation to buy, you may cancel at any time, even after receiving just your free shipment. Simply complete the coupon below and send it to:

THE READER SERVICE, FREEPOST, CROYDON, SURREY, CR9 3WZ.

EIRE READERS PLEASE SEND COUPON TO: P.O. BOX 4546, DUBLIN 24.

NO STAMP NEEDED

Yes, please send me 4 free Silhouette Desire novels and a mystery gift. I understand that unless you hear from me, I will receive 6 superb new titles every month for just £2.40* each, postage and packing free. I am under no obligation to purchase any books and I may cancel or suspend my subscription at any time, but the free books and gift will be mine to keep in any case. (I am over 18 years of age)

D7XE

Ms/Mrs/Miss/Mr _____
BLOCK CAPS PLEASE

Address _____

_____

_____ Postcode _____

RACHEL LEE

◇

A FATEFUL CHOICE

**She arranged her own death—
then changed her mind**

*"Ms Lee's talents as a writer are
dazzling. Put this author's name on
your list of favourites right now!"*
—Romantic Times